4-77

EXERCISE

HOODWINK

EXERCISE
HOODWINK

❖❖❖❖❖❖❖❖❖❖❖❖❖

MAURICE PROCTER

HARPER & ROW, PUBLISHERS
NEW YORK AND EVANSTON

EXERCISE

HOODWINK

1

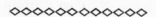

The hamlet of Kingsmead had only recently been enclosed within the boundaries of the great, greedy,
growing city, and it was still pleasantly rural. Factories,
shops, and blocks of flats were scheduled, but as yet not
a sod of grass had been lifted.

However, the tiny village was unfortunate enough to
be beside a main road which entered the city from the
southeast. The new boundary sign was at the beginning
of a bend where the road emerged from a wood. The
bend looked easy, but it was clearly marked: "Dangerous." The finding of a wrecked car at this bend was
the beginning of happenings which ultimately became a
matter of concern to police chiefs of two continents.

Acting upon information received, Constables Hapton
and Marsh of the Granchester City Police arrived on the
scene at 5:35 of a cloudless Saturday morning in early

October. They climbed out of their Wolseley patrol car and looked at the wreck without enthusiasm, because they had been on duty all night and had hoped to be able to go home to bed at six o'clock.

Marsh was a man who seldom grumbled, because he had long since come to the conclusion that when there was no getting out of a job, then it might as well be done as cheerfully as possible. Hapton was less experienced, and though normally of a tranquil nature he was still a little inclined to grouse when he was told to do something today when it could perhaps more conveniently be done tomorrow.

Both men ceased to think about unwanted overtime when they saw what make of car it was. "Cool" said Marsh. "It's an Aston Martin."

At first there did not seem too much wrong with the car, but when they moved round to look at the damage on the near side they saw that it was indeed a ruin. "Five or six thousand quid gone for a burton," Marsh commented.

"Yes, it looks like a write-off," Hapton agreed. "I wonder what happened to the driver."

"He was lucky if he walked away from a bash-up like this," his colleague rejoined. He looked at a row of cottages a short distance away. They were the beginning of Kingsmead.

"Happen somebody in one of those cottages is giving him a cup of tea," he suggested.

Temporarily he was the driver of the police car, and it was his duty to stay with it. Hapton knew all about that. He said, "I'll go and see," and set off toward the cottages.

As invariably happens to men on Nights, the coming of daylight had banished any tendency to be sleepy. As he walked along, Hapton reflected that this was the best time of day. The air was like wine, the sun would be up in a minute or two, and the birds were singing as if it were springtime. "This weather's got them birds kidded," he surmised.

He also reflected that it would not take a man very long to make inquiries at every dwelling in this place. At the farther end of the cottages there was a public telephone kiosk, near to the forecourt of an inn. Next to the inn were the premises of the village grocer-and-postmaster. Farther along were two more rows of cottages, and opposite the inn was a small church and a vicarage. Except for a small wooden cricket pavilion in the field behind the vicarage, that was the whole of Kingsmead.

There were seven cottages in the first row, and all but the last one had drawn curtains. Hapton decided to try the last one first. It was right beside the telephone box. A man without the necessary threepenny piece to make a call might go to the cottage nearest the box.

Before he reached the cottage the policeman saw the herald of the day for city dwellers. Rolling sedately from the direction of Granchester was the first double-decked bus of the morning. It stopped by the inn and reversed into the forecourt, then emerged to face the way it had come. The driver and conductor alighted and lit cigarettes. They looked curiously at Hapton as he approached.

"Mornin'," said Hapton.

"Mornin'," replied the bus driver. "What's up? Lost your scooter?"

Hapton hooked his thumb over his shoulder and said: "Car run off the road back there. Hit a tree or two. Proper mess. Driver seems to have cleared off."

The conductor glanced at his watch. "Let's go and look," he suggested to his mate.

They strolled away. Hapton turned away also, and he had his hand on the cottage gate when the door opened. A man emerged, and turned to lock the door behind him. He was short and sturdy, about sixty years of age. The suit he wore was old and soiled, and so was his cloth cap.

Hapton waited for him. "Mornin', dad," he said. "You're up early."

"Aye. I catch first bus every mornin' bar Sunday. Got to be at me work by a quarter past six."

"You're a timekeeper or summat?"

"Aye."

"What time do you get up?"

"A quarter to five. I like to have time for a good breakfast."

"Did you hear any bangin' an' crashin' this mornin'?"

"Aye."

"See anybody knockin' about?"

"Aye."

Hapton brought out his official notebook. "Tell us about it," he suggested.

"I heard a proper clatter while it were still dark. It must-a woke me up. I put light on an' looked at clock. It were just turned half past four. I put light out an' laid there, but I couldn't get back to sleep. So about twenty-to I got up an' turned me alarm off, an' looked out o't'winder to see what mornin' were like. There were a man in telephone box, telephonin'. Well, I didn't see as I had time to stand there watchin' him, so that's all I can tell you."

"You didn't see or hear aught else?"

"No, that's the lot."

"Thanks," said Hapton. He noted the man's name and allowed him to go to the bus. He made no more inquiries, but went back toward the wreck. The police had been told about that by a night haulage driver at 5:15, and not at 4:40. The man seen using the phone box must have been the driver of the Aston Martin. No doubt he had been asking some friend in Granchester to come and pick him up. So he couldn't have been badly hurt. Probably he would turn up later in the day to look at the damage, but in any case he would be easily traced. Because of this, Hapton had not even asked for a description of the man.

He found Marsh making notes, while the busmen made comments about the broken car. It had been a smart vehicle, with a streamlined saloon body of gun-metal gray. Now it reclined sadly against a very large beech tree. The tree had suffered least in the collision.

The bus driver moved forward saying: "What's it like inside?" Marsh looked up and said: "Don't go tramping around there. We don't know what this is yet."

Hapton was surprised, because Marsh was not an officious man. The bus driver shrugged, and went away with his mate.

Marsh closed his book and pocketed it. "I didn't want that chap nosing in there," he said.

"Did you find any likely cause of the accident?" Hapton wanted to know. "Was it speed?"

"Well, he was traveling a bit. He sideswiped a big tree back there and kept going till he hit this one. But these Aston Martins can take corners as if they were glued to the road. There's a blowout, near-side front. It could have been done during the smash, but I'm inclined to think it was the cause of it. What did *you* get?"

Hapton told his story. Marsh listened in astonishment, and finally exclaimed: "He went and phoned just like that? I don't believe it. Here. Look here."

He walked round and opened the offside front door of the car, and invited inspection. "See that?" he said.

"If he didn't lose a gallon of blood you can call me Dr. Crippen."

The interior of the car was upholstered in light-gray leather, but there was not much of that color to be seen on the front seat. Hapton stared in awe at the gory sight. Then his eyes narrowed. "Most of this blood is on the passenger seat," he said. "There were two people in the car. The driver phoned for an ambulance, I expect. Happen the ambulance had been an' gone before the lorry driver came by an' saw this lot."

"Happen you're right," Marsh conceded. "We can phone the ambulance depot, just to be knowing."

Hapton stooped and peered. "What's that under the dash?" he asked.

"I *think* it's a portable radio receiver."

"It's a big 'un for a transistor set," Hapton commented, taking a closer look. " 'Xavier,' " he said. "Never heard of it."

"I have, though it's the first I've seen. They're an American job, very special. That thing there cost around three hundred quid if it's the model I think it is. It'll perform like Jodrell Bank, that will."

"Well, if he can afford a few thousand for a car he's not goin' to bother about a hundred or two for the sort of radio he wants. But I'm surprised he left it there to be pinched."

"I did touch it, with my gloves on," Marsh admitted. "He left it there because he couldn't get it out. It's stuck."

Hapton looked again. The Xavier appeared to be jammed between the crushed near-side bodywork and the massive clutch housing of the Aston Martin.

"Ah, well," he said. "If you've got your particulars we'll go and get signed off. The Early Turn can take over this job."

"I'd better talk to Headquarters first. It won't take a minute," Marsh said. He went to the Wolseley and contacted HQ by radio. The call took him much longer than a minute. He returned to report: "They phoned the ambulance people. There's been no call from Kingsmead or anywhere near it."

"Ah, well. It'll straighten itself out. Let's go."

Marsh was the senior man. "I've got bad news for you," he said. "I've a feeling there's something funny about this car. The dashboard cupboard and every other receptable in the car is empty. Even the ashtray. It looks as if somebody took just everything there was and stuffed it in his pockets in a hurry."

"So what?"

"So we've both got to stay here till the Early Turn comes out to take over."

"And they won't hurry," said Hapton in disgust. "We've got to hang on here just because of an empty pigeonhole?"

"No," Marsh replied. "Because of a right lot of blood and no body."

2

The scarlet Northwestern Line buses which run over the Pennines between Granchester and Bradford usually are single-deckers. But on Saturdays the company sometimes puts double-deckers on the route if passenger traffic is heavy. So it happened that on Saturday afternoon a man sitting on the upper deck of a bus on the moors beyond Boyton had sufficient elevation to see a human figure lying in a little hollow not far from the road.

The day had fulfilled its early promise. The man lying in the heather could have been taking his ease in the sunshine, but he was in such an utterly collapsed attitude that the man in the bus had other thoughts. He decided: "He looks like a dead 'un."

He thought about that for a little while as the bus

went on its way, and his opinion was strengthened by the realization that there had been no car or motorcycle waiting anywhere near the man in the heather. He went downstairs and spoke to the conductress, a young woman. When she had heard the story and decided to stop the bus, it was more than half a mile from the "body." She alighted and went round to talk to the driver, and the man from the upper deck, whose name was Whiteley, went with her.

The driver was a middle-aged man of much experience on the road. He listened to the story and looked skeptical. He remarked that he was driving a bus, and had to work to a timetable. He also said: "On this road I'll have to go another couple of miles before I can turn back. What are you going to do? Walk back to this here body?"

Whiteley was a simple man, but he was not simple enough to get himself marooned miles from anywhere. He said: "If you stop when you see a bobby, you won't be delayed more than a minute."

"As you wish," the driver said curtly, and the journey was resumed.

In a village called Ripponden on the other side of the moors the bus driver saw a West Riding police patrol car standing at the curb. He stopped his bus close behind it, and Whiteley alighted and went and spoke to the uniformed man sitting in the car.

"At the top of the moors?" the policeman asked when he had listened. "Would it be this side of the county line?"

"I think so," he was assured. "I remember we'd passed the boundary sign."

"Could you show us where it is?"

Whiteley hesitated. "Well . . ." he began.

"Where are you making for, Bradford?"

"No. I'm only going as far as Halifax."

"We'll get you back here," the policeman said. "There's plenty of buses from here to Halifax." And without further discussion he leaned head and arm out of the car and signaled the bus driver to go on his way. That person drove away grinning, his thoughts almost visible. By the time the coppers had finished with that fellow there wouldn't be much of his Saturday left, and he'd wish he'd minded his own business.

"Get in the back seat," the policeman told Whiteley. "My mate'll be here in a minute."

Quite soon another P.C. appeared, pushing his notebook into his breast pocket as he emerged from a shop. As he opened the door of the car he saw Whiteley and asked: "Who's this, er, gentleman?"

His colleague told him. "This gent has seen another gent asleep in the heather, and he's afraid he isn't going to wake up."

The man in the heather was dead, and his injuries were such that survival would have been a miracle.

"He looks as if he fell off an airliner," one of the West Riding men commented.

"He took a high dive and forgot there was no water," said the other one gravely.

"Could he have been dumped here by a hit-and-run driver?" Whiteley suggested.

Both officers had thought of that possibility even before they had seen the body. They complimented the other man on his sagacity and said that he was likely to be right.

When the divisional police surgeon arrived he dryly confirmed that the unknown man was dead. His preliminary examination disclosed severe head injuries and fractures of both legs and hips. Somehow the femoral artery of the right leg had been severed, and the doctor remarked to the coroner's officer that no doubt this injury had bled the man's life away.

A second examination at the mortuary revealed that the man was five feet nine inches long and of medium build. He had no birthmarks or old scars, and he was judged to have been something over thirty years old. His suit bore the label of a tailoring firm with shops in every town, and his bloody underclothes had been bought at an even better-known chain store. His socks and shoes could have been bought anywhere. There was nothing hand sewn about the man. He made a very positively anonymous corpse.

The pockets of the suit contained some loose change, some Gold Flake cigarettes, and a plain white hand-kerchief. There was no lighter, no wallet, no paper money, no letters or documents of any kind. The police took the view that the hit-and-run driver had also been a thief.

The body was photographed, but the condition of the face was such that no newspaper would risk offending its readers by reproducing it. The photograph appeared in police circulars and communications. The usual in-quiries were made concerning both the body and a pre-sumably damaged car. The fingerprints were checked at Wakefield and Scotland Yard, but it seemed that the dead man had had no criminal record. For the time being he remained anonymous.

There the matter rested. The West Riding police knew nothing about a wrecked Aston Martin in the Granchester police district. The Granchester police were making discoveries about the Aston Martin, but they did not connect it with the seemingly obvious victim of an unreported accident whose body had been found seventeen miles away, in another county.

On that Saturday in October no slightly or severely injured driver appeared to claim the Aston Martin, nor did he send a representative. The car had a London registration number, so Inspector Miller of the Granchester Police Traffic Department got in touch with the Metropolitan Police with a view to finding the owner. In due time the Metro checked the number with him, and then told him that it was the number of an Austin 1100 owned by a respectable fishmonger in Camden Town. When consulted, the fishmonger had volunteered the information that he had had to apply for a new Road Fund license about six months ago, because the one attached to the Austin had been lost or stolen.

The news that the Aston Martin was a "wrong 'un" caused Miller to have it examined more thoroughly. No policeman had touched it without gloves, and a search for fingerprints produced the information that there were none. "It's been wiped off" was the verdict.

This discovery was made on Sunday afternoon in the A Division station yard, and it at once led to a search for engine and chassis numbers. It was now expected that these would have been erased, and other numbers hammered in, but it was found that this had not happened. "I'm sure these numbers haven't been touched," Miller declared. "It's a cool and cheeky type who's been using this car. He just didn't bother to change the numbers."

"Probably he didn't have a log book, anyway," suggested P.C. Marsh. He was now off duty, but he had enough of a proprietary interest in the "case" to be watching developments closely.

"Very likely. A stolen car with a false registration and no log book, and no owner if the driver happened to see a copper having a good look at it. All right. We'll get in touch with the makers first thing in the morning. We'll give them these numbers and they'll tell us who first bought the car, and we'll get the real identification number. Then we'll get to know where and when it was stolen."

"That'll be one job cleared, sir."

"Yes. But it'll probably be a Metro job."

It was now almost a certainty that the car's Road Fund license would be "wrong" too. It had been found on the floor of the car still intact in its waterproof cover, though the celluloid front of the cover was quite opaque with dried blood. Miller telephoned the forensic laboratory, but received no answer. Well, it was Sunday afternoon. He allowed Marsh to take the license to Sergeant Bird, A Division's handy man and fingerprint and photography expert.

Bird carefully took the license out of the cover and put it under ultraviolet light. He studied it briefly. "The name of the make has been altered," he announced. "It looks as if 'Austin' was rubbed out and 'Aston Martin' written over it."

"That tallies with information we have," Marsh told him. "This license was pinched from an Austin eleven hundred."

"So I'm not helping you much."

"You never know, do you? When you went over the car for dabs did you notice that big transistor set under the dash?"

"Sure. It looks a bit special, but it won't be any good now."

"It'll be smashed up inside. It must have shot down under the dash when the car hit the first tree. It occurs to me, with it being stuck next to the clutch housing, they wouldn't be able to wipe it off."

"You mean there'll be dabs on it. Why not? Why not get it out?"

"I'll ask the inspector if I can use a jack on the body."

Marsh returned to Miller, and received permission to remove the Xavier radio from the car. With the clutch housing as a base, he used the jack to push back crushed bodywork and release the radio. He carried it to Bird, holding it by two corners with gloved hands.

The sergeant studied it before he touched it. There had been a long glass panel along the front of the set, and that had broken and flown somewhere. But the polished casing seemed to be undamaged. He went to work with an insufflator and found many fingerprints on both ends of the casing.

"There's loads," said Marsh in elation.

"Can't tell yet," he was told. "Nine out of ten will be no good, as usual."

Prints overlay prints. Many had been spoiled in the withdrawing of the hand. But Bird found four perfect specimens: all four fingers of the right hand. He photographed these and left the Xavier untouched until he had developed his pictures. With that done, he returned to the set.

"Xavier," he said. "That's a new one to me. VHF, UHF, the lot. Quite a job."

"Yankee," said Marsh. "They cost plenty. Hundreds."

"I wonder what else it can tell us." The sergeant tried various controls, but nothing happened.

"If they cost hundreds of pounds, they won't sell 'em by the million," he said. "We might be able to trace something or somebody by the number."

"Put the American police on the job?"

"I don't think we'll need to. There's sure to be a main British distributor."

"Who do we know who might tell us?"

"Old Pellman in Holland Street has been in the trade as long as anybody. We could try him."

Bird found Pellman's home telephone number, and spoke to him. The conversation was brief. Pellman did not stock Xavier receivers, and he did not know the name of the distributor. But he was not entirely without information. He knew somebody who had purchased a Xavier set at Harrow's store in London.

Marsh carried this news to Inspector Miller. "Harrow's, then," Miller said. "We'll have the Metro look into it in the morning. I want all the numbers you can find on the set."

Pictures and details of the Xavier fingerprints were transmitted to Scotland Yard and to the County Police C.R.O. The first replies were negative.

"No form, sir," Bird reported to Miller. "Not known at all."

But one hour later Scotland Yard came on the line again. The Metro naturally filed away details of all un-identifiable fingerprints sent to them. A clerk filing details of the Xavier prints noticed some exactly similar classifications on the same page of the index. These similar prints had been submitted the day before by the West Riding police.

Miller at once called Wakefield, and read off the specifications to a clerk there. He waited, holding the line, until he had received the information he wanted.

He told Marsh and Bird: "Your Xavier was handled by the fellow they found dead on the moors. So it looks as if he was lifted out of the Aston Martin and carted up there and dumped. That's another job we've cleared up for another police force. Did you and Hapton go back to Kingsmead and get a description of the man seen in the phone box?"

"Yes, sir. It isn't much. Tall, broad shoulders, dark hair, dark suit, no hat. Face not seen. Also we looked in the phone box for blood. None there. Do you think it'll be any use if Sergeant Bird does the box for prints?"

"A public phone box, two days after the call? I can tell him to try, but he won't find anything."

When Miller said that he was looking at the morning's informations from the West Riding police, he said: "The dead man was of medium height and build, and anyway he couldn't have been standing in a phone box with two shattered legs. So now we know for sure there were at least two men in the Aston Martin, and one of them had a friend somewhere around here who didn't mind turning out before five in the morning and moving a body around. Everything about this points to a slight hitch in a real crook job. I wonder what game they were on."

3

"This is more like it," said André Vidor, stretching his legs from an armchair. His accent was unlike any other in the United Kingdom, and yet it was not what is usually called a foreign accent.

The handsome, red-haired girl leaned on the mantel and surveyed the living room of the new flat. It was furnished comfortably, and almost luxuriously. But she seemed to be unimpressed. "It ought to be, at fifteen pounds a week," she said, and her speech revealed only a trace of her northern English upbringing.

"We couldn't live in a bed-sitter forever," she was told. "And besides, who's paying for it? *You* can't grumble."

She shrugged, and he reflected that nowadays she was quite often in a sullen mood. Perhaps, he thought, she was one of those whose manners were not improved by good fortune. Or maybe she lacked the nerve to be involved in the game he was playing, though her involvement was usually slight. From time to time she had been more involved in more dangerous affairs without making a murmur of objection, but this one seemed to scare her. Perhaps it was the scope of it, as if the amount of loot mattered more than the actual crime. Or perhaps the accident was still bothering her. She had carried on as if it had been murder. Women looked at things in a funny way.

"What will your, er, partner say?" she wanted to know.

"You mean he'll think I'm taking it out of the club? He can't. He looks at the books too closely. He watches everything, either with his own eyes or somebody else's. I wouldn't even *try* to diddle that fellow."

"He'll wonder where you're getting the money."

"Let him wonder. It's no skin off his nose." When he made that remark, Vidor seemed to be thinking of something else.

"If he smells easy money, he'll try to cut in."

"He'll smell nothing, unless you tell him," said Vidor deliberately, because he had been remembering that an hour ago, at the club, she had been all laughter and gaiety. Dixie Costello had been there then; his "partner," who was the real owner of the club.

"Unless you tell him," he repeated. With his head tilted back he looked at the girl, and his eyes were cold enough to make her flinch. He was a tallish, slender man, dark, good-looking, and elegant in his dress. Though he did not have a lot of muscle, she knew that he had a great deal of nerve. Her own thought was that there was not a lot of him, but all there was was man.

"After the times I've stood by you, you ought to be ashamed to say that," she retorted, generating anger in herself because she had known a moment of fear.

He went on as if she had not spoken. "I've been think-ing Dixie could once have been more to you than just a pal of your brother."

Color flared in her cheeks. "That's ridiculous. I was only a kid when I left this town. He must be twenty years older than I am."

"What of it? *I'm* fifteen years older. When you met me you said you liked older men."

"That was just a line. Though I did like you, and I've proved it many a time." Then, womanlike, she attacked with seeming irrelevance. "You used to laugh at me every time I mentioned Granchester. Nothing but Juan-les-Pins or Casablanca was good enough for you. But when you found out about my brother you couldn't get here fast enough."

"Well, obviously." When business was mentioned, Costello was forgotten. "Rodge is just the sort of man we need. He's a live wire. We got a flying start here and I suppose it'll always be the main place. But we've got more than Rodge can handle. We shall soon have to be starting up in London or Birmingham. I might get a move."

He had mentioned this before, and now, apparently illogical, she returned to the subject of Costello. "It was you, not me, who chummed up with Dixie."

"I had to pretend to have a job, and he was the man to find it for me. The club is just right."

"You could have opened a club without him."

"I didn't want to put that much money down. We're not staying forever in this town. Anyway, I needed local support, and he gave the whole thing a send-off."

"Well, he'll certainly be looking at the books when your new car is delivered."

"Nonsense," he said, rising to go to a cupboard and

returning with bottle and glasses. "I'm getting it on the never. Anybody can do that."

"Not a new Rover."

"New or old, who cares?"

"Someday you might be sorry you ever met that man."

This irritated Vidor immeasurably, because he was afraid of nobody, and here was his woman suggesting that someone would get the better of him. "What the hell is the matter with you tonight?" he demanded furiously. "Nag, nag, nag."

This time she was not cowed. She was going to have her say. "I don't like the way things are going, that's all. I don't like that London mob your brother is tied in with. And now there's a dead man."

So it was the accident. Becoming more calm, he reflected that he should have known.

"Well, he can't be brought back," he said. "And that London boy cleaned the job up right smart, with a bit of help. You ought to be glad we got away with it."

"With a man dead? And his poor wife not knowing where he is or anything?"

"You know it was an accident. Nobody murdered him."

"She might think somebody did."

"The London end will square things with her. They'll look after her. Anyway, it's nothing for you to worry about. All *you've* got to do is keep your mouth shut, and I wish to God you would."

"I'll keep it shut. Before I open it again you'll be begging me to say something."

His fury returned. "Like hell I will!" he snapped. "I'll give you time to get yourself a drink and get off to bed. And if you don't wake up a bit sweeter in the morning I'll beat you silly."

Sulky but obedient then, she opened a bottle of gin, while he sipped whisky and glowered at her.

As soon as he could get back to London, Jack Mayhew sought out Toffee Thompson at his flat in Bayswater. There was a scowl on Thompson's ruddy face when he opened his door and saw who the caller was, but he said merely: "Come in."

Inside the flat, with the door closed, he demanded: "What the hell are you doing here? You know you shouldn't come near."

"I had to see somebody, and I couldn't go to Pierre, could I?"

"You could have phoned."

"I did. No answer. Anyway, I don't want to talk about this on the phone."

"Talk about what on the phone? Did something go wrong?"

"That's one way of putting it. Tommy's dead."

"What!"

"I had a tire burst going into Granchester. Near-side front, on a bend. I hit a couple of big trees and wrecked the car. Tommy was on that side and caught it all. He never came round and there was an awful lot of blood."

Thompson's eyes were narrow. "You don't look so bad, to have come out of a bang-up like that."

"Bruised and shaken up, that's all. I was wearing the safety belt, and Tommy had just slipped his off. But you can call it a miracle I was able to walk. I got to a phone box. André came out to me and performed like a hero. We got Tommy into his old car, bundled up in blankets because of the blood. Cleaned the dabs off the doors and that, and got away from there. I got good support, I'll say that much. Even the redhead helped, though the poor girl looked a bit sick."

"What the hell did André want to bring the woman on a job like that for?"

"He had to. She was brought up in those parts. Without her he would never have found me."

Toffee seemed to accept that statement reluctantly. He said: "You got the goods out, of course. And the radio."

"We couldn't move the radio. It was down at Tommy's feet, jammed somehow. We hadn't time to fool around with lights, getting it out."

"I'll get you the cash and you can go and buy a new one."

"Why me?"

"I got the first one. Not much sense in going twice, is there?"

"Oh, all right."

"Pierre won't be pleased about losing the set, but he'll get over it seeing as the consignment is all right. Where did you dump Tom?"

"Up on the moors by the roadside. He has no identification in his pockets."

Toffee sighed. "You should have buried him up there. But it should be all right. If he wasn't lying to me, he has no form, so they won't have his dabs at the Yard. What about André's car?"

"It's an old bedstead. He's going to dump it in an old quarry full of water the girl knows of. But he burned the bit of carpet off the floor at the back, and the bloody blankets, and my suit and shirt. He had to go out and get me a new suit off the peg. I was covered in blood. Not my own, thank God."

"Hear, hear," Toffee agreed. "If you'd copped it as well we'd have lost the consignment."

"I'm touched by your solicitude."

"Don't mention it. Did you come back by train?"

"Yes."

"We should be all right, then. We'll have to get a new man in Tom's place, and another car, that's all."

"You forgot something, I think."

"I didn't. You mean Tom's wife. I've been thinking about her ever since you said he was dead. I wonder how much she knows."

"According to him, she knows he's on some game. He had to tell her that much, because of the all-night journeys. But she doesn't know what it is. And she doesn't know anybody who's in it except you."

"Pity she knows me, isn't it? Anyway, I suppose I'd have to go and see her to stop her running to the police about her husband being missing."

"You'll do that?"

"I don't know yet. I might be sticking my neck out telling her I know he's dead, mightn't I? I'll have to see what Pierre says."

"It would be better if you went with a handful of cash and Tommy's love, and tell her he's had to skip out of the country because some mob has marked him for the chop. Tell her she's to wait for him, and you'll bring money from time to time. Then maybe she'll wait and wait till she meets some other bloke, and then she'll decide he's met some other wench."

"I don't know. She's rather special, I believe. Dead straight. I had my doubts when I set Tommy on. I'd sooner have single men. I don't like women around a job at all. That redheaded bit in Granchester is a liability."

"Oh, I wouldn't say that. It was through her they got organized up there. André on his own would still have been floundering."

"That's your opinion. I don't like her."

"She doesn't like you, either."

Toffee's eyes narrowed. "What's she been saying?"

"Not a word. She treats me like dirt and, boy, any woman who doesn't fancy me most certainly doesn't fancy you."

Toffee was not insulted, and not amused.

"You think a bit about yourself, don't you? Let me tell you something. If anything goes wrong with this business it'll be through a woman, and she'll be the one."

"It'll more likely be Tom's wife who throws the spanner in."

"No. She won't be allowed."

"You may not be able to stop her."

Thompson's voice was cold with resolve. "She'll be stopped, one way or another."

4

On Monday morning an officer of the Metropolitan Police made some inquiries at Harrow's store in Knightsbridge, on behalf of the Granchester police. He learned that a Xavier radio receiver bearing the number submitted by Inspector Miller had been sold by Harrow's early in July. It had been a cash sale, and in fact it had been the only actual cash sale of that very expensive model since the year before.

The circumstances of the sale were so unusual for Harrow's that the appearance and manner of the buyer were remembered by a salesman. He was described as a big man in a loud suit, about forty years of age, with a red face and dark hair: an uncultured person who had been thought to be a bookmaker or at any rate somebody connected with horse or dog racing.

In order for the guarantee form to be completed, the

buyer had given his name as A. H. Ashton, with an address in Dulwich. Further inquiries by the Metro officer had established that there was no such address.

This evasion, and the buyer's description, made Inspector Miller wonder if the Xavier set had been used in some sort of betting swindle. He did not quite see how, but he resolved to bear it in mind. The betting boys dreamed up some remarkable ideas from time to time.

The engine and chassis numbers submitted to the Aston Martin factory brought the information that the first owner of the car had been a man called Wilkinson, with an address in Hampstead, London. This resulted in another Metro inquiry, through Wilkinson and a reputable dealer to a man called Haig in South Kensington. Haig asserted that the car had been stolen from his garage in July, he had reported the matter, and a search of police files proved that he was telling the truth. So, whatever the criminal scheme was, it seemed to have been hatched in midsummer.

The inquest on the man found dead on the moors was likely to be inconclusive and, since the Metro did not seem to be interested enough to invite the Harrow's salesman to look at their private picture gallery, Miller did not see that there was anything more he could do. He attached all the relevant reports and statements to the reports of Marsh and Hapton, and had copies made, and copies were sent to the forces and departments entitled to have them.

So it happened that Detective Chief Inspector Martineau of A Division C.I.D., Granchester, found the little file on his desk on Tuesday morning. This was because, in theory, any crime was a C.I.D. matter. But in practice most of the crimes which were concerned mainly with motorists and their cars were tacitly left to the Motor Patrol, nowadays enlarged and given the title of Traffic Department. Normally, therefore, Martineau would merely have skimmed through the file, but Miller had clipped a personal note to it. The note simply said that the facts in the enclosed reports and statements indicated that the stolen car described therein had been used for some criminal purpose in Granchester or elsewhere.

Martineau perused the documents, and was mildly interested. He spoke on the internal line to Chief Superintendent Clay, head of the Granchester C.I.D.

"That file from Traffic, sir," he began. "Have you seen it?"

"Yes. There may be something in what Miller says."

"Can you think of anything?"

"No. Can you?"

"No. I can't connect it with any of our jobs outstanding."

"That dodgy business with the radio set is a puzzler. It could be used by housebreakers to tap in on police frequencies, to get warning of an alarm, but we haven't had any serious breaks lately."

"Only mugs' jobs, sir. No real professional jobs."

"And thank the Lord for that. Anyway, a copy of this lot will be sent to the Yard, and we'll see if they can sort anything out."

"Yes, sir," said Martineau. But he resolved to keep the file close by him, and to look at it occasionally.

A few days later the body of Theresa Snell was found in an open lockup garage in St. Marylebone, London. It was found in the late afternoon by the man who rented the garage, and he was able to prove that he had not been near the place for more than thirty hours, having gone to Yarmouth the day before and spent the

night there. The man was not seriously suspected anyway. He was sixty-six years of age and it was assumed
that Theresa had been the victim of a sex maniac. She
was the sixth woman to have been murdered by stran-
gulation in the Paddington and Marylebone area within
a year. Each murder appeared to have followed the
sexual act, and in each case it had been evident that this
act had not occurred at the place where the body was
found.

In the first five murders there had been other sim-
ilarities leading to the belief that one man was respon-
sible for all of them. Detective Superintendent Ellaby
of the Scotland Yard murder squad had led the investigation of the first murder, so it was almost inevitable
that he should be put in charge of those which followed.

None of the first five victims was a Londoner. Four of
them were from the English provinces, and one was
from Wales. All were young and unmarried, and osten-
sibly they had come to London to work. Police inquiries
into their various careers had revealed their real am-
bitions. All five had been part-time prostitutes, no doubt
hoping that soon they would become fully and lucra-
tively professional. They had been, as a detective remarked, the sort to get themselves done in.

At first it was assumed that Theresa Snell had been a
woman of the same type, but inquiries made it clear
that there was a break in the pattern. Theresa was a
Londoner, and she had lived all her life in the same part
of Paddington. She was well known in that area. The
picture drawn by the evidence of neighbors had no
murky shadings. Theresa had been a jolly girl who liked
a gay Saturday night. But those times had invariably
been enjoyed in the company of her husband, Thomas
Henry Snell. The suggestion of an irregular way of life

had drawn emphatic negatives from everyone who had known her.

Theresa had had no children. The small terrace house where she had lived was deserted. So, where was Tom Snell? Superintendent Ellaby's desire to speak to that man became urgent. Inquiries were intensive, and extensive. But the typical Londoner's lack of interest in other people—maddening to detectives—was very noticeable here. Snell was not a neighborhood boy. He was a Londoner, definitely, but he could have been a product of any one of twenty boroughs. Even Theresa's sisters were vague about this, holding the opinion that he had come from Stepney or Whitechapel or some such place because Theresa had been reticent about it. Well, what did he do for a living? Here again was vagueness. He had changed jobs a good deal. He had been a salesman, mainly. Once he had been in television rentals, as an employee. He had learned all about radio in the Army— in the Signals, he had once said. And one of the sisters remembered then that he had been a radio repairman at one time, somewhere in London.

Came the question: "What is he doing now?" Nobody seemed to know.

Then: "When was he last seen?" It appeared that nobody had seen him for a week or two, or perhaps several weeks. But Theresa had not told anyone that he was away.

"Who were his friends?" Saturday night cronies were not averse to giving information, but they had little to give. They were friends of Theresa, really, and had met Tom through her. It was generally thought that he was a decent fellow, and good company.

No relations of Tom Snell came forward, to make known his background. The War Office provided details of all the Snells who had ever served in the Royal Corps of Signals. These men were traced. Those who were still alive were able to prove that they were not Thomas Henry. This inquiry was widened, and eventually it became evident that the Tom Snell sought by the police had never been a soldier at all. So, indefatigably, Superintendent Ellaby's minions turned their attention to the Navy and the Air Force.

Meanwhile, a search of the Snell home was yielding better results. On the assumption that Thomas Henry had about as many suits, shirts and shoes as the average man, it was judged that he had had little or no personal luggage when he left home. His fingerprints were found on brushes and shaving accessories, but they were checked with negative results, leading to the conclusion that he was not a convicted criminal.

Other "dabs" in the house were found to be Theresa's, a woman neighbor's, and a woman friend's. That was all, until an investigator turned over a chair with polished wooden arms. He blew his powder onto the undersides of the arms, a place which a housewife with a duster might overlook. Just in the two places where a person might grip the arms when rising or sitting down, he found two sets of four prints. One set had been dragged, but the right-hand set was excellent for identification. It was found that the hands of Toffee Thompson had touched that chair.

"Ah," said Ellaby with satisfaction. "So *he's* out of the nick again."

He made it known to certain subordinates that he wished to speak to Mr. Thompson and, while he waited, he spared a little time to think about the man.

William Bernard Thompson was a man in early middle age who had spent not more than a third of his adult life in prison. Considering his activities and his reputation, this small fraction was a clear indication of adroitness and sagacity. His crimes had all been connected with direct larceny, and never petty: jewels, furs, money; cigarettes and whisky by the lorry load. He affected to despise tricksters and fraudsmen. It was known that he disliked violence, but he had been known to resort to it very effectively. When he was not in prison he lived comfortably and well, and it was generally understood that he had quite a lot of money "sided" somewhere. Besides allowing him to live like a man of property, this money also provided capital for setting up big criminal schemes. But he was only reluctantly a financier of crime. He preferred to use someone else's money if he could. His attitude to a prison sentence was that of the truly professional criminal. He accepted it as a tradesman's risk, "did his bird," and made the best of it.

Physically he was big, strong, and ruddy-faced. He talked a lot in a husky, bronchial voice, and yet he was proverbially discreet. He could be humorous in an unsubtle way, but he was one who laughed with watchful eyes. He had earned the nickname of "Toffee" some years before when a really serious attempt to give up smoking—because of his bronchitis—had led to a temporary addiction to sweets, which he had pressed upon acquaintances *ad nauseam.*

This man had left his traces in the home of Tom and Theresa Snell. One or both members of the Snell family had been keeping bad company. Therefore they had criminal possibilities. This pleased Ellaby. When crooks became involved in a murder there was a chance of turning something up.

Within two hours Thompson was brought to Scotland Yard. He had not been hard to find. Part of his life was an open book—the part he wanted people to read.

"Well, well," he said when he was ushered into Ellaby's presence. "What's all this, Super?"

Ellaby's manner was just as easy. "How are you doing, Toffee?"

"So-so." The visitor seemed to be quite unperturbed. "Living on my losses. How are *you* getting on?"

"Oh, struggling. It's a hard life. Where are you living now?"

"Bayswater. Landsmere Apartments."

Ellaby raised his eyebows. "That new block? How can you afford it?"

Thompson laughed. "Easy, if I don't pay the rent. I might move out at the end of the month."

Ellaby smiled politely. Thompson was not that sort of shyster. He was in the money, as usual.

"So what's all this?" Thompson pursued. "I don't owe any rent *yet*."

"Murder."

The other man stared. Then he said: "Now look . . ."

"Murder," Ellaby repeated.

"Who's been done?"

"Theresa Snell. It's been in the papers."

"I don't read murders. Who is she?"

"Who *was* she. You should know."

Thompson appeared to consider the name. "No," he said.

"You don't know anyone by the name of Snell?"

"Well, let me think. I might have used to know somebody. No. Can't say I do."

"Tom Snell. Thomas Henry Snell."

"No. It don't ring a bell."

"Your dabs, Toffee. In his house. Him missing and his wife murdered."

Thompson seemed to be startled. "He croaked his wife?"

Ellaby shrugged, and said: "Where is he?"

"Don't ask me. I'll tell you what I know about this Snell. I was thinking of buying a nice little electrical shop in Fulham . . ."

"Whereabouts in Fulham?"

"Well, not Fulham. That area. I don't want anybody to know just where it is. It's a snip. I'll buy it if I can find a man to run it for me. I got to have that. Fancy me standing behind a counter."

"You wouldn't be able to keep your fingers out of your own till. Don't give me a runaround. It's Snell I want."

"Well, that's it. Somebody told me this Snell was a good boy, cut out for the job . . ."

"Who told you?"

"Somebody I met in a pub. I don't want to drag anybody else into anything."

"All right, go on."

"Well, I got his address in Paddington, and went to see him. I put it to him. Well, I wasn't struck. He was too fly for me. The questions he asked, I could see he'd be running the business for hisself inside a week. So I said I'd let him know. That's all. I came away and forgot him."

"How long were you in the house?"

"Oh, going on for an hour. Him doing all the talking."

"Did you see his wife?"

There was a very slight pause, a hesitation which was noted. "No," Thompson replied. "She must've been out somewhere. I didn't see a woman at all."

"And that's all?"

"That's the lot."

"It won't do, Toffee. Tell me what this Snell looked like, and then we'll go over the whole thing again. . . ."

They went over it again, and again, with negative

results. Toffee Thompson refused to be squeezed. He had his story and he stuck to it. And when he heard the estimated time of the murder he made it known that he had a good alibi. The alibi was quickly checked, and found to be sound. Ellaby had to let him go. For the time being, he hoped.

Then there was news from the forensic laboratory. The condition of Mrs. Snell's body had put the pathologist in doubt about one aspect of the case, but now certain findings had made him sure. The woman had not been a willing party to the sexual act. She had been raped, either shortly before or at the time of the murder. In that respect the Snell crime again departed from the pattern of the other five Paddington murders, but it still remained one of Ellaby's jobs.

5

The search for Tom Snell was suddenly stopped by information from the fingerprint department of the Criminal Record Office. One clerk there was a little behind with his work, but nevertheless he was thorough. When he was filing the details of the prints found on Snell's toilet articles he found that they were identical with the prints of a man found dead on a Yorkshire moor. Snell had died five days before his wife.

Superintendent Ellaby promptly forgot about Snell. He had six murders to clear, and he was ready to let someone else worry about the affairs of a man who could not have committed the last one. But someone in the Metropolitan Police did concern himself with Snell, on the chance that his death and the peculiar circumstances around it might have some connection with his wife's murder. This man was a Detective Sergeant

Horne of Scotland Yard, the man who had handled the London end of the first inquiries from Granchester. He made sure that the C.R.O. had informed Granchester and the West Riding of the identity of their unknown corpse. He also went round to Harrow's store, seeking more information about Xavier radio sets. There he learned that only the day before there had been another cash-and-carry sale of the most powerful and selective portable model which Xavier made. The purchaser had been a man in his early thirties, tall, well-built, well-dressed and well-spoken. He was described as handsome, with a rather pale face, dark eyes, and dark hair. In manner he had been terse, decisive, and somewhat arrogant. The name on the guarantee duplicate was Richard Smith, with an address in Maida Vale.

Horne went to Maida Vale, and found that the address was a lockup shop, a modiste's owned and run by a woman with a staff of two girls. No men were employed there. No Richard Smith was known there. Obviously the name and the address had been chosen at random.

The inspector returned to Harrow's, and persuaded the manager of the radio-TV department to let him take away "on approval" a Xavier model similar to "Richard Smith's." He took the set to Scotland Yard. From there he communicated with a friend and colleague in D Division at Marylebone, because he had once heard him mention that he also had a friend who was a clever and enthusiastic radio ham.

"Why don't you go to our own radio men?" the Marylebone man asked.

"No," said Horne. "Not yet. I don't want a lot of pooh-poohing on this. I want an outside opinion first."

"I see. Well, the man you want is called Eltham,

Hubert Eltham. He lives at Willesden Green. You'll find his number in the phone book."

Horne traced Eltham by telephone, from his home to his place of work. He was a solicitor's clerk at Lincoln's Inn. He agreed to call at Scotland Yard when he had finished work for the day.

At six o'clock that night Horne brought the Xavier set to Eltham in a quiet little waiting room at the Yard.

"Ah," said Eltham at once. "You've got one of those. I hope you didn't have to pay for it with your own money."

"I borrowed it," Horne admitted. "I've got all the instructions here, but I haven't tried it out yet. I thought you might show me."

"What do you want to get?"

"I don't know. But I think there must be something very special about it."

"It's a wealthy radio fan's toy. Properly handled, it will get you any station powerful enough to reach it, even if it can only reach it with a whisper." Eltham stroked the set's polished casing. "A beauty, isn't it?"

"Will it catch police messages?"

"Child's play." Eltham picked up a catalogue and studied specifications. "I know some police frequencies are pretty high, but this will get the lot, always provided it's in their particular area. See here. Ultra High. I wouldn't be surprised to find it can pick up those pocket transmitters they're issuing to the police these days."

"Let's try it," said Horne.

Eltham played with the set, and Horne watched, listened, and learned. The voice of Scotland Yard's Information Room could be made into a shout. There were others. Horne identified the Constabulary voices of Surrey and Kent, and was satisfied. But Eltham wanted to hear a P.C. on his beat using a pocket transmitter. He tried and failed.

"Perhaps there's nobody using one just now," he suggested.

"Could be," Horne agreed.

"They do have them, don't they?"

"In the outer divisions," said the detective reluctantly, because he hated to admit that the Metro was not up to date in everything. "We're still trying out different makes."

"Naturally you'll want the best," said Eltham, and soon after that he made his departure.

Horne made out his report about the Xavier set and a civilian expert's opinion of it. He sent copies to Granchester and the West Riding. And one copy, he knew, would soon be lying on the desk of Chief Superintendent Coulson, the highest ranking police officer with whom he normally came in contact.

The following morning he took the Xavier back to Harrow's. There the matter rested, a little further forward, but still very much a mystery.

Having inspected the scene of a possible operation on the Chelsea Embankment, Toffee Thompson boarded a certain bus at a certain time in the King's Road, and Jack Mayhew got on the same bus two stops nearer the West End. Thus they met by arrangement but apparently by accident, in a part of London where they were seldom seen. The time was between eight o'clock and half past, which they had judged to be the quietest part of the evening for bus travel. Moreover, it was Monday, which they had judged to be the quietest evening. They sat one behind the other on the upper deck of the bus, with nobody near them. And because each had a seat to himself they could sit half turned away from the window.

There was no formal greeting. Mayhew said grimly: "Well, she's been stopped, all right."

"Don't be like that" was the low-voiced reply. "It didn't go the way it was supposed. She wouldn't play along at all. Didn't believe that tale about Tommy having had to skip off abroad. So Whipper was elected to scare the britches off her."

"Whipper!" Mayhew's quiet voice was bitter.

"He seemed to be the man for it, but he got too enthusiastic. He took the britches part literal, and killed her without intending, to stop her squawking. Leastways, he *said* it was without intention. He said he didn't intend to hurt her at all."

"No, of course not. Just to rape the girl."

"Yeh. Well, if the coppers get him he'll carry it all without bringing anybody else into it. Whipper never come copper in his life, and never will."

"I quote you. Him and his not intending. He might not be able to help bringing us into it."

"No. Pierre told him he's not to come near any of us till he's called."

"We'll still be using him?"

"Sure, when the time comes. He's in. We can't chuck him out. And besides we couldn't get a man as good. It's a pity about the girl, but she's no longer a worry. And the coppers will think it's another of those sex murders. The Paddington killer."

"They'll be damn right too. How do you know Whipper *isn't* the Paddington killer?"

"No. He's not crazy."

"Of course he's crazy."

Toffee shrugged. "Well, there it is," he said, reflecting

with relief that he was in the clear. He had made sure of a genuine alibi for the night of Whipper's attempt to quiet Theresa, just in case anything went wrong, and now he congratulated himself for his prudence. He had not bargained on having the police find his fingerprints in the Snell home, just as he had not bargained for a killing. But he always liked to be covered when there was anything happening.

He said nothing of this to Mayhew, nor had he mentioned it to the man from whom he took orders. What his accomplices did not know about they would not natter about.

Mayhew was echoing his remark. "Yes, there it is. And you know how the coppers are with murder. They never close the book."

"I know. But we're stuck with Whipper and *we* didn't do the murder. And we can't have him seen off. It'd make the others start wondering, especially after poor old Tommy's misfortune."

"Don't bring that up."

"There you are, you see. That's your pigeon, not Whipper's, and you don't like it mentioned."

"It was an accident."

"So was Whipper's job, according to him. Something came over him, and he couldn't help himself. The best thing is to forget *both* members of the Snell family."

The conductor came upstairs, and both men were silent, not seeming to know each other. Thompson paid the fare to Trafalgar Square, while Mayhew decided to get off at Piccadilly Circus. The conductor gave them tickets, and clattered away downstairs.

"How is Tommy's replacement getting on?" Mayhew wanted to know.

"Fine, so far. Saving you work, driving hisself and learning the different routes. I keep checking his mileage on the quiet, to make sure he isn't dodging the column. It's time now for him to start getting used to the set."

"What's he like?"

"Right enough. No wife nor nothing. No ties. You'll get on with him all right as long as you don't start the high society lark."

Mayhew laughed. "Me, high society?" he said. "Prisoners' Aid Society is more like it."

"Well, you've never been better off, have you?"

"No. Not if I could spend some of it."

"No!" Toffee was very positive. "We don't flash nothing. That's important. There's nothing the narks notice quicker. Wait till you've made your pile and packed the job in, then you can flash it. You'll be able to buy yourself a Rolls and a judy to go with it."

"That'll be the day," said Mayhew, as Thompson rose to leave the bus.

"You be good, now," he was warned. "Phone me Wednesday at the usual box, usual time."

"Right. Cheerio."

"Cheerio. And don't forget, no flashing the lolly."

6

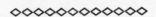

At ten minutes to eleven on the following Sunday night, P.C. 404 Wainman, A Division, Granchester City, was near the end of his first tour of a one-hour night-duty beat. That part of the beat was not one to excite special vigilance: no glittering wares behind the shabby doors and windows of a gloomy little street which seemed to be the poorest in a busy commercial district. But when Wainman found an unlocked door it was an "insecure," no matter how poor the premises. He stopped whistling under his breath when the door opened to his touch, and he made a small grimace when he read the title on the dirty brass plate beside it. The words were: "A. White. Dealer in Precious Stones."

He was young, but seven years in the police had given him a lot of experience. It was not merely a matter of going by the book. Everything had to be taken into consideration, and here was something to be considered. His friend Nobby Clarke had been on that beat from eight to ten before moving on to another one. He *should* have "tried it up" thoroughly. Furthermore, it was Sunday, and Johnny Hurst had worked the beat on Saturday. If this dealer in precious stones had left the door unlocked at, say Saturday noon, and had not been near the place since . . . Somebody could be in trouble. That scruffy little door *could* have been entirely neglected through a night and a day.

Since the issue of pocket radio transmitters the orders about insecure premises had been much easier to carry out. A beat man had only to speak to Headquarters and a colleague would come to him, this being a safety measure not only in a physical sense but also a guard against allegations of pilfering. But there was no struggle between Wainman's knowledge of his plain duty and his adherence to the unwritten code about reporting insecures on Sunday night. "I'll nip in there and see as all's in order," he decided at once. "Then I'll secure it and say naught to nobody."

There were no scratches on the dull metal of the lock, and no splintered wood around it. But Wainman's first doubts came when he examined it. It was a mortise lock, and there was no key on the inside. Still, he was not turned from his purpose. He knew one or two ways of securing doors without locking them.

He stepped back and scanned the windows above. It looked as if A. White had one big room or two small ones over a tobacco shop. Not so important, then. He pushed the door wide open and saw narrow, uncarpeted stairs. He climbed silently, but the questing beam of his flashlight advertised his presence. At the top of the stairs he paused. There was a short landing, with two doors. He listened to the silence of the place. He was used to the dark and to situations of this sort, but something troubled him here. The silence seemed to be loaded with a menace which he could not define. He switched off his light and stood tense. But nothing happened. The silence remained complete, and presently he relaxed.

Still, he slipped his short, heavy truncheon from its pocket and remained in darkness as he felt for the handle of the nearest door. He pushed open the door, and stopped. In the room there should have been a window facing him, but there was complete blackness on all sides. Heavy curtains, then? He switched on his light and saw a desk and a chair and a ripped-open safe, and black roofing felt where the window should have been.

He did not react at once, because all this looked as if thieves had been and gone. With his left hand, the hand holding the torch, he pushed the door wide open, and as far back as it would go. When it stopped, there was no noise of a collision with furniture, nor was there the slight springy recoil of hinges turned to their limits. He guessed that a human shoulder had stopped the swing of the door.

He perceived at once that there could be four or five men behind the door and along the inner wall of the room. The only sensible thing to do now was to leave the premises and, without losing sight of the place, use his transmitter to call for help.

As he turned away there was a small sound behind him, from the direction of the other door on the landing. Someone flashed a light, but before he could turn again his helmet was sent flying by a person who knew the only easy way to do that, by an upward flip of the back brim. This action was immediately followed by a blow on the unprotected head, with a club of some sort. It was so forcefully delivered that no other blow was necessary. The assailant was assured of that by the way P.C. Wainman collapsed and lay still.

A uniformed patrol sergeant, Kennedy by name, waited for P.C. Wainman at his 11:30 P.M. conference point. He waited with growing impatience until 11:45, and then he decided that the constable was not late through neglect. Using his transmitter, he spoke to Headquarters.

"Have you heard anything of four-oh-four Wainman?" he asked.

HQ had not heard from Wainman. A clerk there tried to call him, but received no answer. Sergeant Kennedy made his way to the twelve-o'clock point, and at 12:05 he called the office again. There was still no news of Wainman. He asked to speak to Thornton, the inspector on night duty.

Thornton listened to him, and said: "Stay there. I'll come out to you."

Now, after midnight on Sunday, the streets were almost deserted and motor traffic was sparse; Thornton arrived on foot, because he could walk the distance while he would have been waiting for a car.

"No sign of him yet?" he asked.

"No, sir."

"Very well. We both know the beat. We'll work it, trying all property. You work forward, I'll work reverse, and I'll see you in half an hour."

They did meet in half an hour, but not at the intended spot. At 12:53 the sergeant found an unlocked door, and, eventually, Wainman. And the inspector marched toward the sound of the ambulance siren.

The latest normal C.I.D. shift is Evening Duty: 6 P.M.

to 2 A.M. Also, unless there has been an unusual amount of major crime, Sunday is the Weekly Rest Day of the majority of detective officers. So it happened that on the night of P.C. Wainman's misfortune there were only two A Division C.I.D. men on duty when Sergeant Kennedy's call came. They were Detective Constables Evans and Murray, an unusually phlegmatic Welshman and a deceptively easygoing Scot. Evans was the senior man by a year or so, but both men were experienced and capable. They went to A. White's office in Tingley Street, viewed the damage, and heard the story as far as Thornton and Kennedy could tell it.

"Have you spoken to White yet, sir?" Evans asked.

"No," said Thornton. "I spoke to your D.C.I. He said you should interview White and take particular notice of his replies and reactions."

Evans raised his eyebrows. "Did you suggest the job was faked?"

"No. I don't think it is a fake. One of my men is badly injured, maybe with a fractured skull. I know Aaron White by sight. I don't think he could hit a man so hard."

"But he could have had it done."

"Possibly. But you'll do as Martineau says. It isn't a job you could clear before morning, anyway."

"How true," the detective agreed, looking at an old safe with a ripped back panel.

The C.I.D. men had examined the outer door before entering the premises, and already they had formed a fairly accurate opinion of the circumstances leading to Wainman's injury. That young man's reasons for sticking his head into trouble without first informing his station were understood, and not mentioned. The unlocked door meant that the trouble had been a thousand-to-one chance. There was a telephone in White's office. The thieves had locked themselves in, and when they had emptied the safe they had phoned for their wheel man like calling for a taxi. The wheel man would cruise around the Tingley Street area to make sure that it was safe to stop at Aaron White's door. While they waited for him, the safebreakers had reopened the outer door. Before their transport arrived, they had observed the approach of Wainman, and their door-and-window man had not had time to relock the door with his picklock. But they had had time to conceal themselves, so that if Wainman walked into the premises he would walk into a trap. On reflection, it seemed that the odds against Wainman's bad luck had been much more than a thousand to one.

Apparently there was nothing more to be done in White's office until it had been done over by finger-print men in the morning. A thorough search would follow immediately. In the meantime, there was Mr. White to be informed and interviewed.

"Do we phone him first?" Murray asked, with the telephone directory in his hand. "I've got his number here."

"What's the address?" Evans wanted to know.

"Thirty-two Melbourne Villas, Lea Park."

"We'll go and knock him up, so as we can see his face when we tell him. The Guv'nor said he wanted his reactions."

It was after three o'clock when Evans and Murray signed off duty, and they found a message from Detective Chief Inspector Martineau, to the effect that he would see them in his office at eleven. This time had undoubtedly been chosen because of the regulation eight hours' rest between night and day shifts, a minimum period to which all policemen were entitled, and which C.I.D. men often did not receive.

At eleven o'clock Evans was knocking at Martineau's door. He and Murray entered.

Martineau looked up from his paper work. "Oh, hello," he said. "How did you get on with Aaron White?"

"Not straight up and down, sir," Evans replied.

"No? In what way crooked?"

"I wouldn't say crooked. A bit dodgy."

"Tell me about it."

"Well, we went and knocked him up. He stuck his head out of a bedroom window and I said we were police, wanting to see him on an urgent matter. He said, 'What matter?' and I said it might be something he wouldn't want all the neighbors to know. So he came down and kept the door on the chain till he'd seen our warrant cards. Then he let us in."

"What's he like?"

"He's an untidy old, er, creature, sir. But the house is neat and clean."

"Yes. I'm told he lives alone. I expect he has a housekeeper who lives out. Proceed."

"Well, I told him about the break-in, and he went a bit whiter than he was already. I could see he'd had a shock. I told him the safe had been busted and cleaned out, and he went and sat down. Then he got up and helped himself to a large whisky from the sideboard cupboard. He knocked it back in one, and started laughing."

"Mmmm. Getting you ready for the kid story, eh?"

"We think so, sir. He said the job had been done for nothing, because that old safe had been empty. Then he had another chuckle, but it was a bit hollow. I've seen better actors. He couldn't laugh with his eyes."

"So you didn't believe him?"

"We were inclined not to."

"Did you try to shake the story?"

"No, sir. We let it pass. I asked him if he had anything of value in the office, *not* in the safe. He said he seldom left anything there. He had a better place for keeping valuables, he said."

"I see. Anything more?"

"I asked him if he had a big stock of diamonds or other gems at the present time, and he said: 'I have scarcely any stock at the moment. They certainly picked the wrong time to try and rob me.' He looked a bit shifty when he said that, trying to give us a phony grin. I asked him if anybody might have had a reason to *expect* him to be carrying a big stock, and he said as far as he knew nobody could have had any such reason."

"Did you mention insurance?"

"As a routine question I did. He said he had no burglary insurance on his office, only on his house. He said he dealt usually in small parcels of cheap industrial diamonds, which weren't worth the premiums. When he did have really good stones in his possession, as happened occasionally, sometimes he insured them specifically."

"Only sometimes?"

"That is what he said, sir."

"What sort of accent does he have?"

"A bit of a foreign accent. It's my guess he wasn't born in the British Isles. I'd say a Dutch or German or Scandinavian. I shouldn't think he was born in the name of White. I could have asked him, of course, but I didn't think it was the time and place to go into it."

"Quite right. What does he look like?"

"He must be turned seventy, and his dressing gown and slippers looked nearly as old as that. He was sort of scruffy and clean at the same time. About five foot seven, fairly fat, light eyes, big potato nose; gray hair, none on top and long back and sides. Grayish sort of complexion. He was wearing some of those old-fashioned glasses you stick on your nose."

"*Pince-nez*," said Murray, but not with a French accent.

"He didn't seem to be a bad old sort, sir," Evans went on. "Before we left he offered us a drink. Which we did not accept, sir."

"Would you say he was a man who could get on with people?"

"Oh, yes. Definitely. And not so daft, either."

"Apart from your suspicion of an evasion, did he give you the impression of being honest?"

Evans allowed himself a shrug. "Your guess is as good as mine, sir. He *looked* honest enough."

"All right. We'll have to assume there was no property stolen. But we have a man badly hurt and the job will go on."

The two men departed then. Before he resumed work, Martineau sat a while in thought, about the man he had been discussing. Though none of his staff knew it yet, he had a good reason to be interested in Aaron White, and all men of his kind.

7

◇◇◇◇◇◇◇◇◇◇◇

"No," said Dixie Costello into the telephone. "I can't say I ever heard the name before. I don't know anything about the diamond trade."

"I was recommended to you," said Aaron White.

"Is that so?" The tone was airy and casual. "Who mentioned my name?"

"Perhaps I'd better not say. We'd better talk first."

"Well, I'm a busy man . . ."

"This is business. In five minutes you can make up your mind, take it or leave it. I'll come now, if you like. I know the place."

"All right. Come if you like. I'll be here for the next hour."

Costello put down the receiver and turned to the tall, redheaded girl who was pouring herself a drink at the

51

sideboard. "Popsie," he said. "Get yourself dressed and go out and do some shopping, or something."

"What with?" she asked, without turning her head.

"What do you do with money, eat it?" he demanded.

"You gave me a measly fiver, I can't remember when. Did you expect it to last forever?"

Dixie liked a girl to have a bit of spirit. He grinned as he took folded notes from his pocket. "Here's a tenner, then," he said. "See what you can find to waste it on."

She put down her glass, took the money without thanks, and disappeared into the bedroom. Dixie looked at his watch and realized that it had been a long siesta. She was a hot piece, this one. He decided that he had better not keep her too long, or his health would break down.

He looked around the big, comfortable living room of his flat, and decided that it was in a fit state to receive a crummy little half-inch diamond dealer. It probably reeked of sex and perfume and liquor but who cared? He had no uneasiness as he wondered what White could have learned, and what he wanted. Dixie had walked on the high parapet of danger too often to be worried by mere possibilities.

When the girl had gone he went into the bathroom and made himself presentable, looking into the mirror at a strong, handsome face with a ruddy whisky tan. Well, the whisky hadn't hurt him yet. He drank a lot of it without losing his physical or mental poise. He reflected that he could carry corn, he could. Stamina, that was what it was.

He put on his white silk dressing gown with yellow embroidery, pierced and lit a big Romeo y Julieta, and went to the sideboard. He looked at the four fingers of gin which Popsie had poured and forgotten, and shook his head over both the drink and the girl. No, she wouldn't last long, he was afraid.

Then the doorbell rang. He opened a window and looked down, and called an invitation, and Aaron White came wheezing up the stairs. Dixie had known his name and had known him by sight for a long time, but he was not prepared to admit that. Not yet at any rate.

"So you are Aaron White," he said as the man came into the room. He did not try to shake hands, but added, "Sit you down," and sat down himself.

"Yes, I'm Aaron White," the old man agreed. "And you still haven't heard of me?"

"Not that I know of."

"Ah. Well, I came to see you because I have been robbed."

"I thought you went to the police for that sort of thing."

"The police know my safe was opened, but they don't know what was in it."

"What *was* in it?"

"Forty parcels of industrial diamonds, of various qualities. They average twenty-five carats to the parcel. They'll be hard for the thieves to sell."

"Why *don't* you tell the police?"

"I would never get my diamonds back."

"Well, *I* can't get them back for you."

"I thought you might try. I bought well. It is still worth my while to pay a fence's price. I understand that to be a fifth or a quarter of the market value."

"Were the diamonds insured?"

White shook his head sadly. "Insurance people want to know too much before they insure diamonds. And, anyway, I work on too fine a margin to pay premiums and show a profit."

"What were the diamonds worth?"

"To some people they could have been worth as much as ten thousand pounds, but they're not worth a thousand to a thief with no connections in the trade. And if he does happen to know a fence in the trade he might not get much more than that."

"And what would you give for their return?"

"I'm prepared to give two thousand pounds. That way I could recover at least some of my loss."

"Who told you to come to me?"

"To tell the truth, nobody. I've heard about you. I thought you might be interested."

"For two thousand?"

"If you can get the stones for a thousand or fifteen hundred, you'll do very well out of the deal. From what I've heard of you, you might even get them for nothing."

"Always supposing I could find 'em," said Costello, and then he was silent as he considered all the angles of the offer. Eventually he asked: "How do you know they'll be the same stones?"

"If they're similar they'll do. They're not gemstones, you know."

"Where did *you* get 'em?"

"I'm a dealer. Naturally I don't reveal my markets."

"You bought 'em straight?"

"It was a good buy. I paid less than I might have done, but I paid good money all the same."

"That's what they all say. How do the coppers know your safe was busted?"

"A policeman found the break-in."

"How did they get in? And how was the safe done? Tell me as much as you can."

Aaron White told him, and he listened with an effortless concentration which went some way to explain his high position in his very low profession. He was a criminal and a mobster. If there was anything to be got for nothing—these days, nothing petty—Dixie would try to get it. He was a thief and a murderer. He would blind a man for money.

Nowadays he had certain legal business interests, mostly in connection with gambling. He owned several night clubs. Some people were inclined to forget his dubious past, as people do when a man is rich and occasionally generous. Few people perceived that his every generous act was calculated.

"So they brained a copper," he said when the story was ended. "The cops are still working on it, then, even though they think there was nothing to be lifted?"

"I don't know. They searched thoroughly, looking for clues, I suppose. They did not tell me what they found, but there has been no arrest."

"Has it occurred to you this might not be a local mob at all? Where did the stones come from?"

"I don't know. I bought them locally."

"Only you and the seller knew about the deal?"

"That is right, unless he told someone."

"He sold them cheap. He might have thought he'd get 'em back cheaper. He might have steered a mob to you."

"That is possible. But I've known him a long time. I trust him as much as I trust any dealer."

"Which isn't far, I'll bet." Dixie's voice had hardened suddenly. He went on: "You're not kidding anybody. You're here because you think *I* stole your diamonds."

White was taken aback. "Why should I think that?" he asked feebly.

"You had about a hundred quids' worth of industrials pinched about a year ago. I heard all about it. I have ways of finding out what the coppers know."

"But I never told the police."

"I know you didn't. But they got an anonymous letter giving details of the job saying I'd done it. A hundred quid in rough stones! The police knew damn well it wasn't me!"

"I didn't send the letter. Why would I, when I hadn't reported the robbery? I'd simply have been making a fool of myself."

"That makes sense. But you told *somebody* about the job."

White was silent. Costello went on: "The man you told tried to do me down, and he made the police suspicious of you, because they're always suspicious of people who are afraid to report robberies. And I'll bet the same man mentioned my name to you. Happen he thinks I robbed *him* at some time or other. Half the crimes in this town are laid at my door, but the police aren't daft. They come after me fast enough when they think I've done a job. I didn't do your first job and I didn't do your second. If I wanted diamonds I'd go for something bigger than you ever had. You can take it from me it wasn't my boys who busted your safe. They don't do jobs like that without me knowing. Do you accept that?"

White stared at his hard, composed face, and then said: "I suppose I'll have to."

"Good. As far as my information goes the police aren't *actively* suspicious of you. So now we've cleared the air we can talk business. A safe trade channel is always worth keeping open, and I expect you're as keen to make a bit of money as I am. If I do come across some diamonds, I don't see why I should give you the benefit of the doubt and assume they're yours. You said yourself that any old stones would do just as well. So let's make a deal on other terms. If I bring you diamonds, will you give me fifty percent of the trade price for them?"

"Fifty percent for stolen diamonds?"

"Not directly stolen. Er, *obtained* from people who daren't call the cops. It's safer that way. So what do you care?"

"In those circumstances, I might give you thirty-five percent of trade price."

"Forty. Not a penny less."

"Very well, forty. My valuation."

"Valuation by agreement. I wouldn't argue about a pound or two, but I wouldn't let you diddle me. I know roughly how much a carat you have to pay for good industrials."

"All right. I accept that."

"You'll take any amount?"

"Any amount."

"Good. We'll have a drink on it." Dixie moved to the sideboard, and with his back to his visitor he asked casually: "Who was this bird who sold diamonds to have 'em stole back?"

"Why do you ask?"

"So's I can investigate him, of course. You want diamonds, don't you? If he's getting 'em illegal, we might be able to do something with him."

"I see." White hesitated, and then said: "It was Hervey Crube."

"I thought so." Dixie put a tray on a table at White's elbow. "That's a name you don't forget. Was it him who put it to you that I'd done the other little job?"

White was silent.

"Don't be afraid. I won't have his head knocked off. The thing is past and gone, but I want to know what I'm doing."

"Very well, if there'll be no violence. Yes, it was Hervey."

"If you hadn't told me, I'd have taken it as read." Dixie picked up a glass. "Cheers."

"Cheers," said White, not at all cheerfully. He was afraid of this man who seemed to know so much, and who had so easily "conned" him into giving the name of his old acquaintance Hervey Crube, even though Hervey's actions did not seem to have been entirely creditable. White welcomed the prospect of cheap diamonds taken from people who were themselves dishonest, because business had not been good lately. His best customer no longer seemed to be interested in the sort of industrials he could supply, and of course the recent robbery had been a big loss. This man Costello might make money for him, but he would never feel easy in his company. There was something pitiless about him.

Even now, he thought, Costello was grinning behind a composed face. Everything he had said about two diamond robberies could have been the truth, or it could all be lies. And however that might be, probably he did not care very much whether or not he was believed.

Said Dixie: "I expect Mr. Crube told you not to mention his name to anybody when he tried to make me the goat."

"He asked me not to. He was afraid."

Dixie nodded seriously. "He needed to be. But don't you worry. I won't lay a finger on him. I'll only give him financial cramp in both pockets."

P.C. Wainman was recovering in hospital. There was no fracture of the skull, but the doctors were of the opinion that he would suffer from bad headaches for a long time. His memory was unimpaired, but what he could remember was not illuminating, and indeed had already been surmised by Detective Constables Evans and Murray, and their superior officer Martineau.

Nothing of any use to the police had been found in Aaron White's office. On the safe itself there were clear marks of the chisels and wrenches used, but all had been instruments of a common sort. The assumption that no property had been stolen took the investigators along paths which petered out; no evidence, no loot to seek, no flash money to look out for, nothing to arouse the cupidity of informers.

In the circumstances there was no point in keeping two good men exclusively engaged on the case. But Martineau kept it in the minds of his squad, bringing it up at odd moments so that in the stress of other duties it was not altogether forgotten. He had his reasons for this. A year ago there had been an anonymous letter about a diamond robbery which Aaron White had not reported, and now there had been another robbery and White claimed that nothing had been stolen. The two incidents led to a natural suspicion that White had been in possession of diamonds whose source he did not wish to divulge. And this was happening at a time when the higher ranks of that force and other forces were under official pressure because of a much more important diamond case about which the junior ranks had not yet been informed.

8

The diamond affair which was causing agitation in certain official minds had been brought to light by the Diamond Syndicate, which handled the importations of South African diamonds into Great Britain. At a time when British engineers were very busy indeed, somebody noticed a discrepancy between supply and manufacture. Many more diamond tools were being made for the British home and export markets than had been made a year ago, and yet there had been no increase in legitimate sales of industrial stones. Furthermore, to a lesser degree, there appeared to be a discrepancy between the amounts of rough gem diamonds imported and the amounts of finished gems being put on the market by the diamond polishers of Amsterdam, Antwerp, and London.

Brazilian diamonds seemed to be the answer, at least

in the matter of industrial stones, but consultation with both H.M. Customs in Britain and the Brazilian government showed that quotas remained unchanged and that actual legitimate imports were slightly down.

The Syndicate did not panic. Its directors instigated a thorough private survey and were quiet about it until they knew its findings. The small, highly specialized trade in synthetic industrials was easily checked, and no irregularities were found there. Undoubtedly the discrepancy was in real diamonds. Eventually the figures came, and they were alarming. Moreover, they were conclusive. Diamonds had been and no doubt still were being smuggled into Britain in comparatively huge quantities. Comparatively, that is, only because of the truth of the old saying that you don't find diamonds as big as bricks.

All this meant that great holes were being torn in H.M. Custom's tight control of diamond imports, about which the Syndicate was concerned but not heartbroken. The Syndicate's great worry was loss of trade, and probably actual loss of diamonds at the source through large-scale jiggery-pokery or simple theft. Theft of diamonds by the bagful? It seemed more likely that somebody had a secret mine. Nevertheless, the Syndicate began to give its heads of Security a shaking up of unprecedented vigor.

The results of the survey were submitted to H.M. Treasury and the Home Office, a happening which showed at once the great difference between the business mind and the official mind. For trade reasons the Syndicate was somewhat averse to publicity, but high officers of government turned pale at the very thought of it. If the newspapers got hold of the story . . . Oh dear!

Then how to handle the matter? Only at high level,

of course. H.M. Customs chiefs were informed in admonitory terms. All chief constables were informed, with strict instructions as to secrecy, and no policeman below the rank of inspector was to know anything about the matter at all. This left higher officers of the police asking each other how they could keep a secret and make inquiries about it at the same time.

The great industrial centers of the country were selected for special pressure. Granchester was one of these, in the middle of an area where there was much engineering of all kinds; light and heavy, in factories great and small.

The chief constable was directed to find out what he could about the diamond trade in Granchester, without letting any nonpolice person know the exact nature of the inquiry. He passed this directive on to his head of C.I.D., Chief Superintendent Clay. Clay sniffed over it and made a few dry remarks to himself. He passed it on to Detective Chief Inspector Martineau of A Division, because he happened to be in the same building and was available.

"If you ask me, this is a Customs job," he said. "I don't see much point in us wasting a lot of time over it. But you'd better ask around a bit in a discreet way. Start a file. Just to be able to make a show of having done something."

Martineau's first inquiry was at Northern Steel, a huge concern with many subsidiaries. *Somebody* at Northern Steel would be able to give him a background knowledge of the uses of diamonds in industry. He telephoned an acquaintance who was a works manager.

"Does Northern Steel use diamond-tipped tools?" he asked.

"It does" was the prompt reply. "We also have a firm which makes them."

"I need to get a bit of an idea about the business."

"Aha. Has there been a big robbery?"

"Sorry. I'm afraid I can't tell you about that. For a special reason."

"I see. Hush-hush. Well, the stuff could be in this town. There's plenty used around here. The man to tell you about diamonds is Arthur Burr. Are you in your office?"

"Yes."

"I'll get through to him and ask him to phone you."

Ten minutes later the chief inspector was talking to Burr, who was the production manager of Northern Steel Diamond Tools. "What is it you want to know, Inspector?" Burr asked.

"As much as I can about diamonds. First of all, I'd like to get an idea of the market setup in industrials."

"How would a man get rid of a load of stolen stuff? Who'd buy it?"

"Something like that."

"Well, he'd have a problem if he was just an ordinary thief. He'd have to know a crooked dealer or a crooked toolmaker, and there aren't so many of either. All the toolmakers I know get their diamonds through the Diamond Syndicate, directly or through a licensed middleman. Those are the big firms. There will be some small firms here and there which might get diamonds from irregular sources."

"You mentioned cutting. Do the diamonds have to be shaped before they're put in a tool?"

"In some cases, yes. For certain jobs. But generally the natural points are used as much as possible, especially for grinding tools. Where there is cutting, it isn't anything like the job you see on a gemstone, but it's a skilled job nevertheless. The reason why a toolstone isn't any good as a gem is sometimes because of its color, which might even be black, or because it is cross-grained and impossible to cut like a gem."

"Are there different grades of toolstones?"

"My goodness, yes. They're classified in a number of ways. They can vary in price from thirty shillings to thirty pounds a carat, according to what they can be used for. Some of them we don't use at all. They're throwouts."

"What do you do with those?"

"An old fellow called Aaron White buys ours. He buys our boart too, because we don't use much of it."

"What's boart?"

"Small stuff, used for cluster tools. A number of little diamonds in one head. A lot of it is unusable, of course."

"What does Aaron White do with it?"

"I don't precisely know, but I think we can take it for granted that he sells boart and throwouts to firms which make inferior tools."

"Inferior tools for rough work?"

"That I don't know. *We* don't do any rough work. I should think they're exported."

"America?"

"Not on your life. I'd say Egypt or Indonesia or some place where they don't know what day it is, engineering wise."

"I suppose such toolmakers could be a market for stolen diamonds."

"Undoubtedly, if they were dishonest enough to buy them."

"What about stolen stones which need cutting or shaping? Would a small firm be able to do that?"

"It's unlikely. But if they have a billhead and they are in the business they can always send stones to a cutter without raising suspicion. There's one in this town. Hoosemanns, Brown and Company do a certain amount of our work."

"And there will be other cutters up and down the country?"

"Sure, though I don't know how many. They're in the London region mostly, with offices in the big engineering centers."

"So things shouldn't be *too* difficult for a thief if he knows a shady diamond merchant. Are all merchants licensed?"

"No, but the Syndicate will supply only licensed dealers. That's what the license is for, really. The unlicensed dealers have to get their supplies where they can."

"Does Aaron White have a license?"

"I never asked him. But he usually carries one or two gemstones about with him. It's possible he does have a license."

"I'd like to know who buys your throwouts from him."

Burr laughed. "I doubt if he'd tell you. I did once mention it out of curiosity, and he turned round and asked me if I was after cutting out the middleman."

"Not very trustful."

"No. But he's not a bad old boy. Not that I'd care to buy one of his gemstones."

"I see. Well, thanks a lot. I'm not *quite* so much in the dark now. Could I drop in on you sometime and have a look?"

"Certainly. I can let you see what we have: premier toolstone; first, second, and third quality; boart; octahedrons; macles; ballas; carbonados and so on: there's a job for every stone. Then if you do come across stolen stuff you might have a bit better idea of what you're handling."

"I'll be seeing you then. And thanks again."

"Don't mention it. Pleased to be of some help."

Martineau put down the receiver and sat in thought. Apparently the diamond business was not as small and closely integrated as an outsider might suppose it to be. It was an industry. The difficulties of a thief with uncut stones on his hands did not seem to be insuperable.

And the name of Aaron White had cropped up again.

Days passed, and Martineau discreetly pursued the diamond inquiry when he was not busy with other matters which he considered to be more important. Gradually he built up a file of not very vital information. He thought about the Aaron White jobs. He heard the name of another local diamond dealer called Hervey Crube. But he did not interview either White or Crube. The time for talking would come when he had some definite knowledge on which to base a question.

Then there was an incident thousands of miles away from England, and the diamond affair suddenly came to life. Martineau found himself engaged on the biggest police job in which he had ever taken part.

9

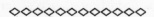

The South African police had not been explicitly informed of the Diamond Syndicate's concern about smuggled stones. It was not necessary to inform them. They were perennially interested in illegal diamond buying and smuggling. In mining and shipping areas it was one of their main preoccupations. In the investigation of such matters they were as ruthless as their ethics would allow.

Lieutenant Hubert Kropp, of Walvis Bay, had served his early years in the police in and around Kimberley. He was an I.D.B. specialist of much experience. Many a gallon of water had he poured on the hard earth floors of native huts, ready to dig at any place where the water seeped quickly away. Many a successful trap had he set for unauthorized merchants who seemed to be unduly interested in diamonds. Many a dusky ear had he probed, or any other suspect orifice. Prehensile brown toes had often been made to uncurl and reveal plunder. Lieutenant Kropp knew all the dodges. Also he had that invaluable attribute which some policemen develop: a sixth sense about people engaged in matters wholly illegal or not quite legal. Something so small as a slight hesitation or a shifting glance or an uneasiness betrayed by hands or feet could start him sniffing, and this in situations where no crime had been apparent or suspected.

For two years he had served in Walvis Bay, the port of South-West Africa, without detecting a single diamond offense. The little town seemed to be so "clean" that it was unbelievable, and his suspicions increased rather than diminished. He could not forget that the coastal edge of the Namib Desert, stretching four hundred miles southward from Walvis Bay to the Orange River, contained two of the richest diamond areas in the world. Offshore, diamonds were taken from the sea. A few miles inland, mighty mechanical shovels lifted aside the deep sands of the Namib to lay bare the diamond-bearing gravel beneath. No I.D.B. in Walvis Bay? Kropp did not believe it.

Naturally he was inclined to be most suspicious of those whom he least understood, and Tiago Diaz was high on his list. For some time he had been telling himself that Tiago was playing some deep game, and if Tiago had known of this thought he would have sailed away to his native Angola at once. Though Kropp might find Tiago an enigma, Tiago thoroughly understood men like Kropp.

In spite of this comprehension, Tiago did not have Kropp's peculiar awareness. The two men knew each other only by sight and reputation, and when they passed in the street they usually did not seem to see each other. But when their glances did happen to meet, Tiago's was as fearless and direct as Kropp's. This irritated Kropp. In his way of thinking, no Portuguese in Walvis Bay had a right to be so little afraid of the police.

Tiago was still in his thirties and in good physical condition. He was supposed to have had some sort of scientific education, but he never hobnobbed with the teachers and doctors of the town. He spent his leisure in the company of other Portuguese in dingy bars. And yet he never seemed to get drunk or to consort with colored girls. In Kropp's opinion, this was not natural behavior for a seagoing Portuguese.

But the chief peg on which Kropp's suspicion hung was Tiago's occupation. He owned a twin-engined cabin cruiser called *Maria*, and he collected marine specimens for biological research. These he sent away to various universities, and presumably this was his living. His range was from the Skeleton Coast to the coast beyond Lüderitz, and sometimes he was away from his home port for as long as three weeks. Around Lüderitz were Diamond Areas No. 1 and No. 2. They were forbidden territory and forbidden waters to any person who did not have a permit to visit. In his quasi-scientific capacity Tiago did have such a permit. To give such a document to a brandy-swilling Portuguese seemed like lunacy to Kropp, but he was much too ambitious to criticize openly the men of power who had granted it.

Tiago's boat was his home and his laboratory. Kropp always gave it a specially searching glance whenever he passed its berth. At times when he was not busy he longed for an opportunity or an excuse to board and search it. But he was not given a chance. Legally, at any rate, Tiago seemed to be a model citizen.

This was the state of Kropp's mind with regard to

Tiago when the S.S. *Ismailbaksh* called at Walvis Bay. The ship was a 10,400-ton freighter of the United Oriental Steamship Line, of Karachi. She anchored out in the bay, and only her English captain and her Scottish chief engineer came ashore. Kropp discovered that the reason for the call was commutator trouble. The *Ismailbaksh* would remain at anchor until new parts had been flown from Capetown. Two days at the very least, he surmised.

Despite the fact that the ship remained out in the bay, where any visit to her would be noticeable, both police and customs felt the need to be vigilant. They had learned that she came on this voyage from Chittagong, via Calcutta, Colombo, Mombasa and Capetown, and was now bound for Europe with jute, oil cake, and castor seed. Well, India was the Mecca of gold smugglers, and the Orient generally a source of narcotics. The commutator trouble could have been deliberately caused by a member of the engine-room staff. There was a possibility that drugs might be smuggled ashore at Walvis Bay, and gold or diamonds smuggled out.

Night was the time of greatest police vigilance, and at first darkness Kropp himself picked a spot along an open quay within sight of the *Maria*. He was not specially thinking about Tiago, but that was the place he chose. Under the deep eaves of an odorous, single-story fishmeal warehouse, his khaki uniform and sunburned face were invisible at seven yards. And he knew the first principle of concealment: he stood quite still.

The night itself was still, and away beyond the tidal disturbance there was smooth, starlit water around the ship anchored out there. Kropp watched the water, as he watched everything else in sight.

More than two hours passed, but Kropp did not move.

He had the patience of a born hunter, and he was not conscious of boredom. When a darkly clad figure flitted past the other end of the warehouse which sheltered him, his pulse quickened just a little as he perceived that this newcomer was heading for the *Maria*. But he did not move.

There was a light in the *Maria's* main cabin, but there had been no movement on the boat since night-fall. Kropp saw the dark newcomer hop aboard, and he seemed to be carrying a bulky parcel. Tense now, Kropp scarcely breathed.

There was more light from the *Maria's* cabin as the door opened briefly to admit the visitor, and then Kropp began to wonder if he *was* a visitor. Was it Tiago himself, merely bringing home a parcel of groceries? So furtively? It was possible, but unlikely.

A minute later the question was answered. The visitor—presumably the same man—reappeared, and went away as silently as he had arrived. Kropp had not a hope of recognizing him, but his shadowy outline and the style of his movement told the South African that he was not wholly Bantu or Hottentot. "Another damned Portugee," he decided.

His glance returned to the *Maria*, and he was warned by a very slight change in its outline. The difference was a very small protuberance on the line of the gun-wale. It had not been there before. Kropp was sure, because he had been looking at the boat for two hours. He guessed that he was seeing the top of a man's head. Tiago was on deck, as immobile as the policeman who watched him.

"If my damned sergeant comes now," Kropp vowed silently, "I'll have his guts for my breakfast."

The sergeant did not come. The small roundness breaking the *Maria's* clean outline disappeared after a minute or two. The single mast rocked a little more as someone moved about the boat. Light appeared and vanished as the cabin door was opened and closed. Kropp moved then, silently in shadow, to the other end of the warehouse. When he was directly opposite the *Maria*, he again became as still as a cat waiting to pounce.

Five minutes later the cabin door opened again. Someone emerged, but the light was not extinguished. Kropp discerned in starlight the strong, classic shape of Tiago, an outline ruined by the oxygen cylinders on his back. Also, he seemed to be carrying something big enough to fill the crook of one arm. Before the policeman could make a decision about his own next action, Tiago stooped and went quietly over the side.

So Kropp remained still. There was no hurry now, and the man in the water might still be watching from under the stern of his craft. No, there was no need for haste. Whatever Tiago was taking out to that ship could be found before she sailed. Tiago himself would be met on his return. Kropp grinned in the darkness. That Portugee wouldn't be so damned cocky when he realized that he had been under observation.

Ten minutes later Kropp went aboard the *Maria*. As he had expected, the cabin door was not locked. Tiago would not carry his keys on an undersea operation. In the cabin the owner's white shirt and khaki linen trousers were thrown on a bunk. Lying in the other bunk was a shark club, or "billy." Nothing else of interest could be seen. Kropp went forward, and then aft. Soon he had searched the boat. There was nothing to excite him. Anything incriminating which Tiago had he had it with him.

The policeman thought about the scavenging sharks around the ship out there. He knew that men like Tiago were not afraid of sharks. Usually they swam too deep to be prey to them. But Tiago would have to surface to get his bearings before he reached the ship, and he would have to surface *at* the ship. And yet he had not taken his shark billy. Perhaps, Kropp thought hopefully, the club in the cabin was a spare one. He did not want some hungry fish to rob him of Tiago.

He went on deck and made himself comfortable while he waited. But even now he did not allow himself the luxury of a cigarette. The boat moved very gently under him, a movement that a hand reaching up from the sea would disturb considerably. When that sudden rocking came, he looked in the right direction and saw the fingers and knuckles of a brown hand on the gunwale. Then another hand and an arm appeared, holding a large adjustable spanner. Before the spanner was put down on the deck, Tiago's head appeared. With a miner's lamp on his forehead, his goggles and his face piece, he looked like some monster from the deeps of the Atlantic. The goggles did not prevent him from seeing the service revolver under his nose. His chin shook and his teeth chattered, but that was not fear. The icy Benguela current flows past Walvis Bay.

"Come aboard, Senhor Diaz," Kropp said softly. "Come aboard before I blow your head off."

What Tiago Diaz suffered at the hands of Lieutenant Kropp is not on record. Since the policeman had no real evidence at the time of the arrest, it may be assumed that his treatment of his prisoner was extremely artful or very drastic, because the man eventually did confess that he had swum out to the *Ismailbaksh* with a parcel whose contents had not been disclosed to him. He said that he had put the parcel, wrapped in waterproof plastic material, into a basket lowered from the stern of the ship by someone whom he had never seen or spoken to. The basket would be there, he had been told, and all he had to do was to put the parcel in it and silently go underwater again.

Kropp smiled, and picked up the spanner. "I thought maybe you had to attract his attention by knocking on the ship's plates with this."

"I couldn't find my shark billy. I took that instead."

"Don't lie any more. Your billy is on a bunk in the cabin. I saw it myself."

Tiago was silent. Kropp sighed, and said: "It looks as if I'm going to have to start all over again."

"If you kill me I can't tell you more than the truth."

"I *will* kill you if I don't get it. Come on; what about this monkey wrench? It's big enough for—for anything. It looks like a shipyard tool to me."

Tiago did not seem to be listening. He was sunk in misery and pain.

"Who visited you just before you went over the side?" Kropp asked. "Was he the one who brought the stuff?"

Tiago shook his head. Kropp considered him, and saw his predicament in its entirety. He went on: "They'll kill you if you come copper. Is that it?"

Tiago nodded, and the nod was a mistake. It confirmed Kropp in his opinion that the really important information was yet to come. But after sitting in thought for some time, he did not continue the inquisition. He left Tiago under guard, feeling sure that the Portuguese was a small pawn in a big game. The game was the thing. He wanted to be alone for a while in order to do some real hard thinking.

10

Tiago's future, immediate and distant, was dark indeed, and he was left to contemplate it for two hours while Kropp worked hard to better his own.

For Kropp, there were defects in the present situation. There was, for instance, a time element. He assumed that he could *eventually* screw the whole story out of his prisoner, but if the man was in fear of death for betrayal, it might take some days. And already, or in the morning at any rate, somebody would be waiting to hear from him that his undersea operation had been successful. Then, probably, it was intended that the good news would be passed along the line to the boss man. If there was no such news, and no sign of Tiago, everybody would be alerted, and it might even result in a warning going out to the *Ismailbaksh*. The contraband would be thrown overboard, and Tiago would have no case to answer, and Inspector Kropp would look like a blundering fool.

Bearing all that in mind, the policeman weighed the chances of breaking up a big criminal operation, and rounding up a whole herd of smugglers, including the boss man. Also his glance returned constantly to the big spanner now on the table in front of him. A dockyard tool? What the devil had Diaz wanted with that?

He thought objectively and systematically about the spanner, and at long last he had an idea. With a strong glass, under a strong light, he examined its fine-toothed jaws. Paint, he thought, and a bit of rust, and tiny fragments of marine shells. Barnacles, limpets, what have you. Limpets! He grinned, and carried the wrench back to Tiago, and carefully laid it on the table in front of him.

"I think this is going to be more serious than I.D.B.," he said. "There are Indians on that ship out there. The Portuguese haven't forgiven India for the Goa take-over. This is political, isn't it? You stuck a homemade limpet bomb on that ship, and somehow you needed this wrench to make it fast."

Tiago was startled. "No, no!" he cried. "Not a bomb!"

"What, then? You'd better tell me. It can be found, you know."

Tiago realized that the police would be able to bor-row the services of the port authority's divers. "It *is* a sort of limpet bomb," he admitted. "But there is no ex-plosive."

"It is loaded with what?"

"Diamonds."

"Diamonds! Gemstones?"

"A few, perhaps. But mostly industrials."

"Bah, they're not worth the trouble."

"High-grade industrials. Around fifty rand a carat."

Kropp calculated swiftly. There were more than two thousand carats to the pound weight. At fifty rand or seventy dollars or twenty-five pounds sterling a carat. If this so-called limpet held only one pound of diamonds . . . Phew! And it might hold much more than that. This was a big game. Somebody was aiming to make millions out of it. Even the educated Senhor Diaz would only be a pawn in a game like that.

"If they're graded they're not merely pilfered by diggers. It's an organized job."

Tiago shrugged. "I don't know."

"Is anybody on the ship mixed up in this?"

"No. Nobody knew it was going to call here."

"Did you fasten this thing to a condenser inlet?"

"No. I clamped it on the starboard bilge keel."

"And it will be quietly taken off at some other port, without anyone on the ship knowing anything about it?"

"I imagine that would happen."

"Which port?"

"I don't know. I am only the delivery man."

Kropp reflected that possibly Tiago really did not know, since there had been no need for him to be told. It was not a matter of first importance anyway. After a chat with a shipping agent in the morning the exact itinerary of the *Ismailbaksh* would be known. There was now a question of whether or not the ship would be allowed to sail away with its unnoticed illegal attachment. That was a matter for Higher Authority. A decision would have to be made as to whether or not the South African police would catch a sprat or take a chance on catching a whole shoal of mackerel.

It was a choice loaded with danger to an official. If it was decided to play the game big, Tiago would have to be given his freedom, to make his report that all was well. He would become, in effect, a police agent. But when he had made his report his work would be done.

Kropp looked at Tiago and reflected rather proudly that there was not a mark on him. A few shots of brandy would make him a man again, for the time being at any rate. He was fit enough to do the job.

"I might be able to let you go," he said. "Play the game with me, and you can get clear of any trouble."

No hope could be seen in Tiago's pained brown eyes. "I'm listening," he said, not hiding his skepticism.

"I mean it," said Kropp. "You don't count. You realize that. If you play along you can get clean away with it, and nobody will know you've even seen a copper. It all depends on whether or not you're already blown."

"Blown?"

"It depends on whether or not you should already have passed the word that you did the job right."

Tiago thought about that. "You're going to let it ride? All the way to London River?"

"London, is it?"

"London is my guess. That's all."

"But you heard something to help you guess, eh? I never heard a Portugee talk about London River in just that way. You may be a bigger fish than I thought."

"No. I'm a nobody." The fear showed in Tiago's eyes.

"All right. Are you blown?"

Tiago hesitated. "No. Not yet. It is in the morning when I go into the town as usual."

"You've done this before, haven't you? It's been a regular thing when London-bound ships called. And then there's been a cable to London, saying Aunt Annie should arrive on such a date, and she's got a tumor on her navel, or a bun in the oven, or something of the sort."

Tiago was silent. Kropp said: "All right, I'm not inter- ested in any of that. *This* is the job I'm interested in. If you'll play along, I'll try to arrange it. I may *not* be able to arrange it, you know. I'm only going to try. If it can't be arranged, you go to jail. If you refuse to play, you go to jail. And I beat the everlasting hell out of you to find out who your contacts are. You can be sure I'm going to find out."

"You say I get clean away. How?"

"Without me there's no evidence against you," Kropp said, and Tiago's glance lingered with hopeless longing on the revolver on the policeman's belt. "I can just tell my bosses that I've had a sure, certain tip-off. If they decide to play, you go about your business as usual. You report that you did the job, which is true, isn't it? You carry on as normal. Scotland Yard and the Thames River police will attend to the matter at the other end. They'll mark the stuff as it goes all the way through, and nail the lot. They'll find correspondence, or an address. That's all we want at this end. Just to *know* who the boss man is will do for a start. *After* we start making arrests I'll pass the word to you, so it'll look natural when you pull out for Angola or Portuguese East or wherever you want to go. You can trust me."

Tiago was very far from trusting Kropp, but the alternative was appalling. If he did not throw in his lot with this big blond beast, he would go to prison anyway. And he would be made to talk before he went. The contraband diamonds would fail to arrive in London River. They were worth many thousands of rand. Tiago Diaz would be in trouble more serious than police trouble.

"First," he said to Kropp, "you will have to talk to your chief, and he will have to talk to his chief. You will have to find out if a deal with me will be allowed."

"That is so. I'll get that moving straightaway."

"Second, a small favor."

"You're not in a position to ask for favors. What is it?"

"The man who came to my boat. He is—a very close friend. You can skip him. He is only the errand boy."

"But I shall want him. I shall want to know *his* contact."

"If I tell you his contact, a more important man, you can skip him."

"H'm. All right, that sounds fair enough."

"Very good. Then it is a deal if you can arrange it," said Tiago, but he did not offer to shake hands on the bargain.

"I believe I can swing it," Kropp replied confidently, and then his eyes narrowed. "If you think you're going to tip off your friends and beat it, you're making a big mistake. If your boat leaves its mooring, it will be stopped. If you go anywhere near a train or a plane, I'll have you inside before your feet can touch the floor. Any move of that sort, and you've had it. You'll stay in town until I tell you you can go."

Tiago knew that Kropp was not boasting. He nodded. "I'll stay in town."

Kropp did not let it go at that. "And the next contact but one? I might as well know now."

"No. I will tell you when the arrangement is made."

Kropp looked at him, and decided to leave that for the time being.

11

For Martineau the job really began with a request from the chief constable's office for Martineau's diamond file to be sent up there. He hastily perused recent additions to the file before he let it go out of his hands.

Half an hour later Martineau himself was called to the Chief's office. He found there the Old Man—who was still of early middle age—the Assistant Chief, and Chief Superintendent Clay. The diamond file lay open in front of the Chief.

"Good morning, Chief Inspector," the Chief said pleasantly. "Do sit down."

Martineau returned the greeting, and sat, reflecting that the expressions on the three faces did not suggest that there was going to be any trouble.

"I see you have been doing something about this diamond job," the Chief went on. "As much as you possibly could, perhaps. I don't think anyone will be able to grumble about us."

"The file contains all that is known by ourselves and the Northwestern Crime Squad. We had nothing concrete to work on, sir."

"That is understood. But in a day or two you might have more information. You will have to go to London sometime today. The Chief Clerk is at this moment looking up a train or a plane and booking you in somewhere for a couple of nights. You have an appointment at the Yard at half past ten tomorrow morning, in the office of the Assistant Commissioner 'C.' "

"I stay *two* nights, sir?"

"I am advised that you should. This suggests to me that it will be a long conference, or several conferences. At any rate, you will probably have a busy day or two. Stay in London as long as the A.C. 'C' requires you to. When you come back, report to your C.I.D. chief, then both of you come here and report to me personally."

"Yes, sir," said Martineau.

"Yes, sir," said Clay.

At twenty-five minutes past ten the following morning Martineau presented himself at the office of Colonel Russell, Assistant Commissioner for Crime in the Metropolitan Police. But he did not go into Russell's own office. He was shown into a conference room adjoining.

The room seemed to be full of big or biggish men. He saw several he knew. There was Chief Superintendent Coulson of Scotland Yard. There were Vanbrugh of Lancashire County, Kirkwood of the West Riding, Finnerty of Liverpool City, Walker of the Northwestern Crime Squad, and MacLeod of Birmingham City: all C.I.D. of rank and experience. He was introduced to

men from Coventry, Cardiff, Glasgow, Leeds, New-
castle, Middlesbrough, Nottingham, Leicester, and
Bristol, and to men of the Midland and other regional
crime squads. Coulson the Yard man seemed to know all
of them.

There was some general talk, some speculative comment, and a few dry jokes. Laughter was subdued. Then
every man rose to his feet as Colonel Russell entered
the room with R.A.L. Henty, a regular "police" official
of the Home Office whose name was known to every
member of the Police Federation.

"Be seated, gentlemen," said Russell. And when the
shifting of chairs was over he went on: "Please smoke if
you like. I suppose most of you know Mr. Henty, or at
least you've heard of him. So we'll just find out if we're
all here, and who's who."

He looked at Henty. Henty was businesslike. "We're
quite a gathering," he said. "I would like each officer to
answer to his name."

He read out names from a list, and each high-ranking
policeman meekly answered: "Here."

"Good," said Henty. "Now I'll see your credentials.
I'll come round and look at each warrant card, and give
it back to the man I got it from."

Russell was not looking amused, so there were no
smiles. Henty checked each name and warrant card
against his list, and was satisfied. Then Russell smiled,
and a few men grinned.

"All present and correct," the A.C. "C" said. "I expect
you all have an idea of why you are here. Diamonds.
The recent Whitehall flap." He inclined his head a little
ironically toward Henty, and Henty made a solemn little
bow in return.

Russell continued: "The chief concern of Whitehall

seems to have been not that ourselves and Her Majesty's Customs should turn up a crowd of smugglers, but that the press and the general public should be kept in ignorance. Well, something has turned up, and we, the police, are even more concerned than Whitehall that there should be no leakage of information. So I would like to make it clear, right away, that whatever is discussed here today must not be discussed elsewhere, except with those of your superior officers who will need to be told. Is that understood?"

There was a murmur of assent, and Russell added: "I expect certain officers of lower rank will have to be informed eventually, but never at any time will we have any unnecessary discussion, *please*."

He waited a moment, and proceeded: "We've had a bit of luck, if the findings of a vigilant officer can be called luck. The South African police have turned up some diamonds for us. They are on the way to London attached like a limpet bomb to the bilge keel of a cargo boat called the *Ismailbaksh*, home port Karachi. The captain and crew of the *Ismailbaksh* don't seem to be in the secret at all. They don't know about this artificial barnacle on the hull. Unless we find evidence to the contrary, we are assuming that they are perfectly innocent.

"The diamonds in their container were attached to the ship in Walvis Bay in South-West Africa. That region used to be called German South-West, but that was a long time ago. Nowadays it is to all intents and purposes part of the South African Republic. Alluvial diamonds were discovered there in comparatively recent years, and now there is a considerable industry along the coast. Diamond diving, dredging or digging, or however it is they get them.

"It was a lieutenant of police at Walvis Bay who learned about the limpet business, and he had the foresight to consult his superiors before he breathed a word to anyone else. One prisoner who had been persuaded to, er, come copper was set free, and we are told that his discretion is assured because if he opens his mouth somebody will cut his head off. The South Africans are prepared to risk losing the bird in hand in order to get a dozen or two from the bush. They are less concerned about losing one parcel of diamonds than they are about failing to catch somebody they call the Boss Man. They have let the *Ismailbaksh* sail with the diamonds, and they are hoping that we can clear the job at this end and find documents or correspondence, or obtain information, which will lead them to the Boss Man. They want to break up an entire organization. Is all understood so far?"

There were no questions, and no one was making notes. But Russell's audience was undoubtedly attentive.

He went on: "I might tell you that there was a very serious discussion about that in this office the day before yesterday. There was some argument. One or two officers did not see how it could be done. They thought we might lose the smugglers *and* the diamonds. But the prevailing argument was that, so far, it had been done, and that it was up to us to follow through. This was not a matter of pride and prestige, it was a matter of sound police work. Also it was a challenge. We are not overlooking the possibility that through some accident or mistake the whole job might be blown, but if that does happen we at least will have the information we have gathered up to that point. We won't lose everything. So, whether or not you fellows approve, we are going on with it. That is the operation we are going to discuss this morning. Any comments?"

Coulson the Scotland Yard man apparently had heard it all before. He said: "Should you give them an outline of our proposed arrangements for the river, sir?"

"Is that necessary?" Russell queried. He frowned in thought for a moment, and then he said: "Perhaps we should." He looked at Henty, and Henty nodded.

"Very well," he said. "Our inquiries on the shipping side have had to be extremely discreet, but we have learned as much as we need to know. The *Ismailbaksh* made a stop for repairs at Walvis Bay, and actually she had no port of call between Capetown and London, where she will discharge castor seed. From London she goes to Hull, to get rid of oil cake and take on machinery. From Hull she goes to Dundee to discharge jute, then she goes across to Gothenburg and takes on more machinery. Thence to Hamburg for machinery, Rotterdam with oil cake, picking up agricultural machinery, and then she sails back to where she came from. We have not yet alerted those ports. We're considering that. If it so happens that this consignment is gemstones for a change, the destination could be Rotterdam. However, we will be ready for all eventualities by the time the ship gets here.

"We don't imagine that the limpet can be detached while the ship is moving, so we are assuming that it will still be in place when she comes into London River. At Gravesend she will come under the jurisdiction of the Port of London Authority, and the P.L.A. will see that she gets a berth which will suit our purposes. She will not be approached or interfered with, except by the usual port officials on routine duties. We hope that she will be able to dock without incident. Questions?"

There were no questions. Russell continued: "Naturally, the ship will be under surreptitious observation long before Gravesend. She will be watched all the way up the river, and if she stops anywhere, P.L.A. or River Police will not be far away. But we are inclined to assume that the limpet will be taken off at night by a frogman. We don't know how he will approach, but we do know he can't swim awfully far under the surface of the Thames without losing his bearings, day *or* night. He will slip over the side of a boat somewhere near or from the riverside equally near. We shall know where the *Ismailbaksh* will be, and we will have lots of time to put our observers quite close and under cover. It'll be a ticklish business, but with infrared cameras and one thing and another we'll get what we want.

"After that there will be the much more difficult business of keeping a boat or a car under constant observation without arousing suspicion. We will have to track those diamonds to some rat hole where the London head of the gang will be waiting to weigh and examine them before he sends them off somewhere.

"If we are lucky enough or clever enough to locate that London boss, the main part of the job will be done, and a great many men will have done an awful lot of work to do it. We are not minimizing either the work or the risk. Nevertheless, if we succeed we are not going to stop there. By fair means or foul we are going to track those diamonds to the receiver. We want to catch the man or men who have made the crime worthwhile. *If* the diamonds are moved out of the Metropolitan Police District, then you chaps will come into the picture."

Russell waited then. MacLeod of Birmingham ventured: "Isn't it possible they'll simply send them as registered mail, sir?"

Russell nodded. "Undoubtedly a possibility. Arrangements will be made with Post Office Security. Every angle will be watched. That is to say, every angle we can think of."

Martineau rather surprised himself by saying: "I have reason to think that they will go by road. And you will have to look out for a switch of cars."

12

Colonel Russell raised his eyebrows. "Already a definite opinion," he said. "From Granchester City, is it? Proceed, Granchester."

Martineau already regretted his impulsive remark. He should have waited and given some thought to the clear idea which had just emerged from a jumble of possibilities. But he had been told to proceed, and he realized that he must make good his preliminary remark, quickly and concisely, before he launched himself upon the involved story which would have to follow.

He began: "Merely an opinion, as you remark, sir. But if smugglers *must* get diamonds out of London to the provinces they will be safest going by road. They are criminals, and members of a criminal organization. They are ruled by fear and self-interest in about equal parts. They are answerable to bosses who only trust them to do what is best for themselves. And what is usually best in a mob like that is to play it straight or be found dead in an alley. They can't insure their diamonds. Therefore, they can't mail them anywhere because in the event of loss the story that they were *really* lost and not sold to somebody would not be believed by the top man. They can't afford to lose them, so they feel safer by road, keeping them in their possession."

He paused before making his next point. He decided to answer the first objection before it arose. "You might suggest that they would be safer going by train, or by air. Certainly those are safer means of traveling, but not for crooks with their names in the form book. A big railway station is not a healthy place for a crook, and neither is an airport. They are liable to be stopped and turned up; or at least they can be spotted, and notification sent to the police at their destination. That sort of thing happens every day, as you know."

He waited, inviting comment. As he expected, somebody said: "They could also be stopped and turned up on the road. In a routine check, for instance."

He shook his head. "Not these people. And I'll tell you why. An unusual happening in Granchester some time ago tells *me* why, though I'll confess I have only just perceived it. I'm afraid you will have to listen until I get back to my original point. Five minutes, sir?"

"Ten," said Russell. "If it gets us somewhere."

So Martineau told the story of the smashed Aston Martin at Kingsmead, and the body on the moors. He mentioned the oddity of an extra, and very powerful, radio receiver in the car. He told his audience of the investigations of Sergeant Horne in London, establishing that the Xavier radio had been bought for cash, under a false name. Still quoting Horne, he explained that another Xavier radio had recently been bought under the same circumstances, by a person of a different description. Then he saw that Coulson and Russell had already perceived the drift of the argument, and he relaxed somewhat.

"Sergeant Horne had one of those sets tested by an expert," he said. "From inside this building he was able to pick up police messages, even messages transmitted in county areas. It seems quite likely to me that *some* valuable plunder had been transported in that Aston Martin, and a man practiced in picking up police messages in every police district through which he passed had been sitting beside the driver listening for news of checks and roadblocks. And of course they had traveled by night because they arrived at Granchester in the early morning. Night travel would be best because there would be fewer messages on the air. They would receive news of police obstructions or checks in good time to turn aside and avoid them. All they wanted was a quiet, uninterrupted journey from one place to another."

"Suppose they were stopped for a spot check?" came the query.

"In that case, I imagine that the man who stopped them would be permanently quietened. I don't think they'd stop at murder."

That remark caused eyebrows to be raised, so Martineau explained: "The man found dead was called Thomas Henry Snell, and we believe he was the radio operator. Recently his widow Theresa Snell has been murdered. It looks like one of the Paddington jobs, but it *is* just possible that she might have been put away because she was too insistent on learning what had happened to her husband. I might add that we associate the husband with the Xavier radio from the car because his were the only fingerprints on it."

Coulson spoke up: "You certainly have a theory, Chief

Inspector. But I understand that an industrial diamond
has to be shaped up before it is put in a tool. That must
be a skilled job. Do you think it would be done in London before being sent out to the provinces?"

"I very much doubt it, sir. The toolmaker himself will
have to decide which diamonds will need shaping for
his purposes and which won't. In any case he must be
in touch with a cutter because he will receive tools
back from his customers from time to time, for worn
diamonds to be reset so that new points are exposed. I
don't think he'll have any trouble about that, since he
is already in the business. He can send diamonds away
to reputable cutters, insured and registered. His billhead won't be queried so long as he pays his bills. I
mean to say, after he has illegally received the diamonds, every subsequent operation will seem to be legal
and normal."

Henty was looking worried. "Could they *really* tune
in to every police district with a Xavier radio?"

"As they drew near to it and passed through it, sir.
I'm told that Sergeant Horne's expert believed that that
particular model would even be able to pick up the new
pocket radios."

Coulson said: "I've seen Sergeant Horne's reports.
Undoubtedly the Xavier radios were purchased by two
separate and distinctly suspicious characters. Also, I
suppose, the Aston Martin was a wrong 'un?"

"Stolen, sir. With false plates corresponding with a
stolen Road Fund license."

"So this journey to Granchester was definitely a
crook's tour, and the only glimmering we have of its
purpose has been produced by Mr. Martineau. I think,
now, we had better see if one or two of Harrow's salesmen can find those slippery Xavier buyers in our picture
books. Incidentally, a character called Toffee Thompson

was interviewed about the Snell murder, but he had an alibi. Still, he must have known Snell. His prints were found in his house."

"It occurs to me now, sir," said Martineau, "that the description of Thompson tallies roughly with the description of the first Xavier buyer."

"Excellent, if it should actually be Thompson," said Russell. "We have a suspect already. Even if Mr. Martineau happens to have guessed wrong about diamonds, I'm sure he's right in surmising that the Aston Martin was carrying *something* very valuable, either smuggled or stolen. And the purchase of a second Xavier radio indicates that other similar runs will be made." He turned to Martineau: "Have you any ideas for beating this obviously crooked gang?"

"Only hazy ones at the moment, sir. I think we shall have to do some hard thinking."

"Only too true. However, we will accept your theory as a possibility, and we'll all give it thought, and discuss it again when we meet this afternoon. Now, the next item on the agenda. Receivers. Your comments, please."

"Unlicensed diamond brokers, for a start," said Finnerty.

"Possibly," conceded MacLeod. "But we mustn't ignore the possibility of licensed merchants giving way to temptation."

There was a murmur of assent, and Vanbrugh said: "The Diamond Syndicate stresses the sheer size of this smuggling caper. There might be a dozen receivers in different cities."

Russell nodded. "And I suppose you all have a few doubtful characters in your sights. But assuming as many as a dozen dishonest middlemen, to where can they move so many diamonds? I have been told repeatedly that reputable diamond-tool firms *know* that their industrials come from the Syndicate, and they won't accept any that don't. So where do these others go?"

A number of men wanted to talk, but Martineau was not one of them. He thought that he had made enough noise for one morning, and anyway his mind was inclined to dwell on the other problem which Russell had posed. It was the man from Birmingham, the greatest engineering center, who eventually took the floor. His information was more or less the same as Martineau's.

"I'm told that there *are* small firms which buy inferior diamonds from shady dealers and make inferior tools for export to the East and the Middle East, where the traditional corruption enables them to bribe government buyers. I'm also told that this business can't go on for long because their engineers are learning fast, and will no longer accept rubbish. We don't know who these small makers are, or *where* they are, and we can't find out without giving the game away with open inquiries, or breaking into offices at night to look at the books. We might eventually be able to make the inquiries, but of course the other procedure is out of the question."

All the other C.I.D. men looked as solemn as Mac-Leod when he made that remark. In dire emergencies, secret and highly illegal searches were very occasionally made by officers breaking the law for what they considered to be the public weal. But in the presence of the A.C. "C" of the Metropolitan Police such matters were indeed out of the question, and as proof of that Russell was looking as solemn as anybody.

MacLeod went on: "If some of these small makers are now getting good diamonds cheap, their sales problems are at an end. They will be able to increase production and take all the stones the smugglers can supply. And if they're buying toolstones really cheap, their profits will be enormous. A diamond tool may not be as simple to make as it looks, but it does look like a simple little thing to me. All the same, it can sell at anything from twenty to a hundred pounds according to the diamond tip. Any maker who is getting a lot of smuggled stones will be making a lot of money, and it's quite possible they will soon be trying to edge into the European or North American markets. With regard to this sort of prosperity, until we have something concrete to go on we can only try to spot these firms by looking for flash money: signs of sudden wealth, little firms working nights and Sundays, that sort of thing. The workers themselves will be innocent enough. Once a suspect firm is spotted, it shouldn't be difficult to trail a few workers to their favorite pubs and listen discreetly to their talk. If they're working with diamonds, they're sure to mention it sooner or later. That is all I can suggest at the moment, gentlemen."

"And a good suggestion too," Russell approved. "It won't do any harm to have a few suspect firms spotted when the crunch comes. Now"—he looked at his watch—"I have an appointment, and I believe so has Mr. Henty. So we'll leave you fellows to talk things over. You can have lunch in the canteen, or go out for it. But I beg you, gentlemen, not to drink enough to dull your wits. We'll meet here again at half past two this afternoon."

Left to themselves, the rest of the gathering talked more freely, and some spoke who had not spoken before. Ideas were put forward, accepted with or without reservation, or rejected. Then Martineau looked at his three old friends, Finnerty, Kirkwood, and Vanbrugh.

"I don't know about you lot," he said, "but I could do with a pint before lunch. If I can find some decent ale around here."

"I know where the ale is," said Walker of the Northwestern Crime Squad. "I'll make one in, if I may."

So the meeting split up on a roughly regional basis,
and the five men from the North went in search of
good ale, which they drank in moderation. Then they
stretched their legs as far as Covent Garden, and had
lunch at the Nag's Head.

They wasted no time while they ate and drank. They
talked business, and when they returned to Scotland
Yard they had the outline of a plan. It was voted that
Martineau should put the plan to the meeting, because
the original need for it had been suggested by him. He
accepted the responsibility without reluctance, because
his brain was hot with the plan and needed ventilation.

"Well, gentlemen," said Russell, when the meeting
had reassembled. "I haven't had much time to think
about our problems, but I hope you have. I think first of
all we should have suggestions in connection with Mr.
Martineau's ingenious theory."

Said Coulson of the Yard: "I'm more and more inclined to think that it is more than just a theory. At least
it looks as if it will clear *some* major crime for us. But
I'm afraid it's going to need some awful smart police
work."

"We can do what we have to do," said Russell. "What
does Mr. Martineau have to say?"

Having much to say, Martineau stood up to say it,
and he did not spare any detail. The meeting listened in
a silence which became almost respectful. When he sat
down the silence continued until Henty, unusually
genial, said: "Well, there you've got it on a plate. Safeguards as well."

"Yes, indeed," Russell agreed. "Congratulations, Chief
Inspector."

Martineau protested that many of his ideas had been

suggested by other officers present. That was agreed to, and noted.

"So," said Henty, still smiling. "What do we call it?"

There was time for thought. Then Coulson said: "It isn't a Metro job, so we can give credit where it's due. How about *Operation Provincial*?"

Nobody was enthusiastic about that. The man from the Midland Crime Squad said: "It's intricate. More threads than a tapestry. *Operation Tapestry*?"

"It'll probably be a night job," said Vanbrugh. "How about *Operation Nightmare*?" Then he added grimly: "It'll be a nightmare for any of my men who don't do the job right."

This hint of old-fashioned discipline pleased everybody. But MacLeod had been thinking along the same lines as his Midland colleague. "*Operation Spiderweb*," he said.

"Now, that *is* good," Russell approved. "Any more?"

Finnerty had been in deep thought. He said suddenly: "*Operation Hoodwink*."

"That's good too," said Russell. "We'll put it to the vote. *Hoodwink* or *Spiderweb*."

Hoodwink won by two clear votes, and then Coulson offered an amendment. He said: "A lot of the men will be obeying orders without knowing the full story. They'll be less inclined to wonder, and talk about it, if we call it an exercise. I suggest *Exercise Hoodwink*."

"Accepted," Russell said. "Any advance on *Exercise Hoodwink*?"

There were no more suggestions. It was agreed.

13

Two salesmen from Harrow's store were invited to Scotland Yard and asked to turn over the pages of "picture books," the pictures being the full-face, profile, and full-length photographs of convicted criminals. One salesman was only asked to turn over a few pages, one of which showed Toffee Thompson at the beginning of his last prison term. Without hesitation the salesman identified him as the man who had bought a Xavier radio in July, paying cash and giving a false name and address.

The other salesman had a more difficult task, but bearing in mind the description of the second Xavier buyer, Sergeant Horne decided to let him go through the books depicting London car thieves. Half an hour is a long time for a man to look at faces, but at the end of that time the salesman positively identified John Morrist

Mayhew as the man who had quite recently bought a second Xavier radio on a cash-and-carry basis, also giving a false name and address.

Mayhew's record was studied, and something of his history was gleaned from notes attached to the reports of his first offense. If there can be such a thing, he was a superior type of habitual criminal. He had been educated at a very minor public school, this school having cost his father as much as one of the "best" schools. He had left school with poor qualifications, but fair marks for mathematics had encouraged the father to article him to a firm of accountants. He was supposed to study hard, but he had a not unnatural liking for girls and a gay time, and he had a consuming interest in motorcars. With money borrowed from his mother he bought a shabby old sports car, and home study was entirely neglected for several months while he tried to make the old car run like a new one.

He was taken to task by his father, and there was a quarrel. Apparently he left home, because he next appeared in London's Warren Street with money in his pocket, and where he got the money was never revealed by his parents. But his father was afterwards so embittered about him that it was surmised he had forged a check which one of his parents had honored to prevent a prosecution.

He was growing into a big, personable young man, with an easy, occasionally arrogant manner, and a way of looking elegant in the most casual clothes. When he spoke, his accent was good. Not that it mattered in Warren Street.

Those were the postwar bonanza days of the used-car dealers, and their claims were staked in Warren Street. Young Mayhew had a sixth sense about cars, and he traded shrewdly. He made money, but he also spent it.

When eventually the flood of new cars made used ones harder to sell, he was an experienced trader. He had also become the sort of driver who could get the best out of any car. But he had about as much money as when he started. When the market became tighter still, he found that he could not compete with men who had been in the business while he was still at school. He began to find it more profitable to sell cars without having paid for them, and without the consent of the actual owners. He did very well at this for a little while, and then he was caught with a stolen Austin, and sent to prison for one year.

He served his time and came out, and through a connection he had made inside he became the wheelman of a "pussy" mob. Unfortunately he became the only victim of a tip-off when the Flying Squad caught him with a carload of stolen furs. He refused to give any information about his associates. Five years in prison was the sentence.

After that he was a hardened criminal, a real crook who saw no other way to live. The days "out" were great days, a life of affluence and excitement. The days "in" were the price he paid for the life he led. He accepted that. He was not a violent prisoner nor was he an escaper.

After reading this record, Coulson remarked to Superintendent Ellaby that he did not see Mayhew as a murderer, though he could have known Theresa Snell through her husband. Still preoccupied with the murders of women, Ellaby queried: "What about his chums?"

"We only know Thompson, so far," was the reply. "And you couldn't break his alibi."

It was not considered wise to have Thompson watched, because his interview with Ellaby would undoubtedly have made him uneasy and vigilant; a hard man to follow surreptitiously. But it was assumed that Mayhew would still be unaware that he was a suspect, and the best men Coulson could find were put on his trail. After two days of careful shadowing, patience was rewarded. Mayhew went to a house in Notting Hill and stayed twenty minutes. The visit was in the afternoon after the public houses were closed, a time when a person of regular drinking habits might be expected to be at home. After Mayhew had gone away, the house was "staked out." In the early evening a man called Whipper Slade emerged. "Coo, he's a real deadleg," said a detective who recognized him.

Slade was thirty-eight years old, and his record was long and bad. He had been given his nickname "Whipper" in boyhood, when he had been a persistent shoplifter. His "form" now included larcenies of many kinds, and such offenses against the person as robbery with violence, attempted murder, grievous bodily harm, and rape. Of the past twenty years of his life, fifteen had been spent in Borstal or prison. And yet he was valued as a club man or "guard" by people engaging in robberies. He was a rather short man with a mean face and narrow shoulders, physical characteristics which sometimes caused people to overlook his very powerful hands, arms, and legs.

The news that Slade seemed to be an associate of Mayhew made Coulson now feel sure that he was nosing along the track of a major crime, because nothing else *but* a major crime would put two such men in contact. Coulson presumed that even in prison Slade's surly crudeness and generally low mentality would cause Mayhew to keep away from him, not from any sort of fear but from distaste. Undoubtedly they had been introduced for business purposes, probably by Thompson, a man who could get on with anybody except perhaps a homosexual. It looked as if Mayhew was now deputizing as liaison man or pay clerk, because Thompson was taking precautions.

While Thompson was still left strictly alone, Slade was put under discreet surveillance, so that twenty-four valuable detectives were now working round the clock on the tailing game, drawn from a section which was short of men in any case. Coulson, now in daily conference with the indefatigable Sergeant Horne, wondered how many more of the gang the observers would turn up.

"There'll be a new radio operator, learning his job," said Horne. "Running over the various routes and noting different police wavelengths."

"Well, Mayhew isn't driving him. Unless he's driving himself, it means they've got two wheelmen. Then if they're the diamond mob they'll need a man who can handle boats, and they'll need a diver. So if you count the headman there are at least four and probably five more members of the mob who are still strangers to us."

"You don't see Thompson as the headman, sir?"

"No. He'll be second in command, I expect. The top man will be somebody who's in touch with South Africa; somebody who knows diamonds. Thompson wouldn't know what he was getting, and he wouldn't know how much to ask for it."

"You mentioned the diver, sir. If we could spot him we'd know for sure it *was* diamonds."

"So we would. Well, it won't be Whipper. I'll bet he even hates having a bath."

"I can't understand what they want with a man like Whipper."

"He's very reliable. He's never come copper in his

life, and he never will. And he can hand out the stick. There's got to be a guard on every big job, ready to stop any interference, without hesitation."

"That's Whipper, all right," Horne rejoined.

Almost by a miracle surveillance on two alert men was maintained for five days without a hitch, and without any observer having a fear that he had been noticed. But undoubtedly much was missed. It was, for instance, considered too risky for either of the men to be followed into public houses, public lavatories, newsreel cinemas, and other possible meeting places. Neither could their conversations from public telephone boxes be overheard. Much was missed, and no other likely member of the gang was spotted. But the S.S. *Ismailbaksh* was drawing nearer to England, and Coulson insisted that there should be no lessening of vigilance.

Trouble blew up when Ellaby learned of Whipper Slade's possible connection, through Thompson, with the Snell family. Ellaby had murder on his mind, and little else, and Coulson called him in just in time to prevent him from having Slade brought in for interrogation. Ellaby insisted that he "had a right." Coulson rather tactlessly gave him a flat order to keep himself and his men away from Slade.

"Six murders," said Ellaby. "They take priority."

"You have no evidence. You can talk to him till you're black in the face and he won't cough. We have him under observation. We'll leave it that way."

"I've a good mind to ask to see the A.C. 'C.' "

"I'll go with you," said Coulson.

They went to see Russell, posing him a difficult question. He pondered, then came down on Coulson's side by deciding that the questioning of Slade would be without result at that stage and that the man was harmless while under observation. "If you had some concrete evidence it would be different," he told the disappointed Ellaby.

Meanwhile Sergeant Horne had been giving a great deal of thought to the unknown man who would remove an attachment from the bilge keel of the *Ismailbaksh*. After delving into records of Thompson, Mayhew, and Slade, he was able to turn to the records of all the men who had stood trial with any of them. He also visited the offices of the Prison Commissioners, and looked at lists of the names of men who had served in prison with his suspects. It was a tedious business, but Horne persevered. The name of any prisoner who had Royal Navy anywhere in his history was noted for special inquiry. With this list of names he went to the Admiralty, and eventually proved to himself that very few of the Navy's divers had turned out to be criminals, and of those few none was a Londoner. Nevertheless, he was thorough, but he sent out his provincial inquiries without much hope. He now had a fear that the man he sought might not be a trained diver at all, but merely a good swimmer in possession of a frogman's equipment.

His next inquiry was at the London office of National Oxygen. After that he went to see Coulson.

"I've been thinking about oxygen cylinders, sir," he said. "Skin divers for the use of."

"Where do these frogmen's clubs get their oxygen?" Coulson wanted to know.

"If they get it in London, it's from one depot in the East End. They can take empty cylinders in good condition and have them replaced by full ones. There is only that depot allowed to bother with small stuff like that. I'm told that most of the customers for that sort of thing are known. P.L.A., the river police, ship repairers, marine insurance people, and the like. They don't get many amateurs."

"So?"

"I might make inquiries there."

"No," was the decisive reply. "You can't trust a civvy not to talk. One whisper that the coppers are interested in people getting oxygen could blow the game to blazes. No. No direct approach."

"As you say, sir. But our clients could be getting their oxygen any time now. Do you think we could stake out the depot for a few days?"

Coulson shook his head. "I haven't the men. And, besides, I'd have to tell them something. You know, Horne, you're supposed to be the only policeman in the country below the rank of inspector who knows anything at all about this diamond lark. If you want to watch that oxygen depot you'll have to do it yourself."

"I may do that, sir?"

"Of course. But I'm relying on you to be careful."

Horne departed, and went home to change into a drab shirt, old shoes, and his gardening suit. From home he went by bus and on foot to an oxygen depot in dockland. He found the depot to be a collection of brick sheds with covered loading bays, in a big yard with high brick walls. In the front wall were two wide gateways marked "In" and "Out." A little farther along the wall was a small door. Across the street, facing the long wall, was a row of shops and other commercial premises. Almost opposite the gates was a big and busy cafeteria, and a little farther along was a workingmen's restaurant. At the corner there was a little inn.

"Everything a man could wish for," he decided.

He walked around the outside of the depot. There was only one more gate, at the back. It was closed and it had a disused look, and a padlock chain was visible, no doubt attached to a lock on the inside of the gate.

"Front entrance only during business hours," he surmised. "Just the job."

He went right around until he was at the front again, and entered the cafeteria. He bought a cup of coffee and carried it to a table not far back from the window, and there he sat and watched the teeming life of the East End go by.

14

About four o'clock the following afternoon Horne was sitting by the cafeteria window when he was approached by a woman who appeared to be the manageress of the place. She came with the air of a good woman determined to do her duty. Horne had been expecting her.

"Good afternoon," he said, smiling, but not rising from his seat.

"Afternoon, sir," she said, because Horne had decided that he need not wear his gardening suit, and he was decently dressed.

"You're wondering why I spend so much time here?"

"That's it. You were here yesterday, and two hours this morning and three hours this afternoon. The girls are uneasy about you."

"I suppose I'd better tell you. I'm waiting for my wife. She left me and I heard she was living somewhere round here. I figured she might come in here, or else she's bound to walk along this street sooner or later."

Compassion struggled with prudence in the woman's expression. "I hope there won't be no trouble?"

"None at all," said Horne promptly. "I'm a peaceable man. Besides, she'll have the children with her."

"Children?" The woman was relieved, and interested. "How many children?"

"Two," Horne lied fondly. "Two little girls, aged four and six."

There was another struggle, this time with curiosity. The woman was wondering how this stranger's wife was subsisting, if she hadn't run away with some man. But she did not quite have the effrontery to ask. She went away and spoke to one of the counter girls, and the girl looked at Horne with sympathy, and thereafter his presence was accepted.

The cafeteria was the handiest observation post, but Horne took his meals in the nearby eating house, and he occasionally had a drink at the corner pub. Four days passed, and he was not troubled. It was probable that word had gone along the street that he was a man seeking his wife. No doubt there had been a few masculine jokes. Men would have been saying: "Blimey, I wish I could lose mine."

A little after eleven in the forenoon of his fourth day's vigil, Horne was sitting over an empty coffee cup in the cafeteria. He saw a man of his own age walk past the window and stand by the curb, waiting for an opportunity to cross the street. He had seen the profile clearly, and now he saw it again as the man looked this way and that. He knew him.

"Mullins, was it?" he pondered. "No. Mullen."

The London Metropolitan is one of the great police

forces of the world. It is an army of law men so nu-
merous that even colleagues who actually know each
other—even men who have served in the same division
together—may actually lose touch with each other completely. So it was with Horne and Mullen. Fifteen years
ago they had both been in the same class of police re-
cruits. For two or three years they had been in H Division together. Then Horne had been given a trial in
the C.I.D. and had succeeded in staying there. And
what about Mullen?

Watching the man cross the road, Horne remembered
with no great certainty that he had joined the police
after doing his national service in the Royal Navy.
Horne's interest rose. Navy men in the force often made
application to join the River Police. Many of the River
Police were trained divers.

The watcher had noticed a light-gray Jaguar car stop
farther back on the other side of the street about five
minutes before. Now he saw it begin to move toward
Mullen, who was now safely across the street and standing by the curb. Mullen was not looking at the ap-
proaching car, but he was certainly trying to take a look
at everything else in sight. Horne knocked his coffee
spoon to the floor, and stooped to pick it up. When he
looked again the car had stopped, and Mullen had
opened the near-side rear door. He lifted out a fairly
large parcel and carried it toward the depot entrance.

Aware now that the driver of the Jaguar would also
be using his eyes, Horne half turned from the window
and with his elbow on the table concealed the lower
part of his face with his hand. He appeared to be once
more looking at the newspaper which he had been
pretending to read for the past half hour. He penciled
the Jaguar's number—YXX 7793—on the margin of the
paper. Out of the corner of an eye he could still see

the car; not clearly, but well enough to see movement near it.

After five minutes of eyestrain he did see movement. He turned his head a little then. Mullen was returning to the car, still carrying the parcel or one very similar. The driver of the car was watching Mullen, and the policeman was able to take a good look at the face of a man whose picture he had recently studied: John Morrist Mayhew. He at once turned away.

Now the car was a gray blur again, but he saw it move off. Mullen was no longer in sight, so apparently he was now Mayhew's passenger. Being in no hurry, Horne sat in thought, about a police officer who seemed to be running errands for a crook. That was bad, very bad.

He left the cafeteria for the last time and returned to Scotland Yard. From there he made a call to the River Police Headquarters at Wapping.

"This is Sergeant Horne, Central Office," he said. "Is Sergeant Lambton on duty?"

"Yes, Sergeant," he was told. "He's just popped into the super's office. I'll ask him to— Hold on. He's here now."

Lambton spoke: "Now then, Billy. What do *you* want?"

"I just wondered how you were getting on. You never drop into the old place now."

"Oh, you'll be seeing me. My boy Jim has had to take on six months' special coaching for his law degree. We can't all have bright kids. It's costing plenty of money. So I've gone teetotal for a while. Stopped smoking, an' all."

"Good for you, my lad. It'll be worth it."

"I hope so. Three months since I had a drag, and I'm still dying for one. How's things with you?"

"Oh, fair. No sickness in the family. Have you still got the same shower in your lot?"

"Mainly. One or two new faces."

"How's my old rookie pal Mullen getting on?"

"Mullen? Oh, Mullen! He brought his clothes in about eighteen months since. Resigned."

"Oh dear. Was there trouble?"

"No, not really. But he wasn't getting anywhere, nor likely to. He had friends, it seemed. He started coming on Late Turn a bit damp round the edges. That was noticed, and sniffed at."

"So somebody choked him off, and he packed the job in?"

"Well, I don't know if he was told off. He seemed to make up his own mind. Said he couldn't live on his pay. I don't blame him for that."

"Nor me. Is he married?"

"Married and parted, the last I heard. That didn't do him any good here, either."

"It never does. Any offspring?"

"No. Not that he was owning to."

"My, my. I don't think you cared for my old mate."

Lambton had not been deceived. "Come off it," he said. "What's it all about?"

"It's about saying nothing to nobody. That means nobody. I just called you to ask how you were getting on."

"All right, if that's the way you want it."

"You keep quiet, and I'll tell you later. Any idea where this ex-copper is living?"

"No. He had to move out of a police house when he left the force."

"I see. Many thanks. I'll be seeing you when you come out of Purgatory."

That was the end of the talk. Horne knew that he

could rely on his friend Lambton to hold his tongue, and yet he had not risked trying to find out if Mullen had been trained as a diver. And really there had been no need to ask. Now that he knew the man had left the service, Horne could ask to see his police record without arousing curiosity.

He went to look, and found that Mullen had attended two diving courses, his marks being noted as "Fairly good" and "Good." This indicated that he would know how to handle an aqualung and its accessories, and no doubt he would be capable enough in the water at the fathom or two's depth necessary to reach a ship's bilge keel.

Horne's next inquiry was in motor registration. He found that the car lawfully bearing the number YXX 7793 was not a Jaguar and was not gray. This discovery was reassuring. The Jaguar which had been used by Mayhew and Mullen was just as "wrong" as the ill-fated Aston Martin had been. It had been used to collect something which could have been a frogman's oxygen cylinder. Horne was moderately sure that he now knew the name of the man who would detach a parcel of diamonds from the hull of the *Ismailbaksh*. He went and told Coulson about it.

Coulson nodded in approval when he had listened. "Good work," he said. "Four suspects now, while the ship is still a thousand miles away. But I'll be happier when we've located this Mullen. I don't like ex-copper crooks. They know too much."

"Will you put out the word for him?"

"Definitely not. He might still have one or two friends in the force. And since the men wouldn't know why we wanted him, one of them might think it would be friendly to tip him off. When we do find him, we won't be able to have him tailed."

"What about the Jaguar, sir?"

"That's different. We'll be looking for it. Position and direction to be reported. Not to be approached under any circumstances. Have you looked for Mullen in the phone book?"

"Yes, sir. There are no male Mullens under his initial."

"What's that?"

"Q for Quentin. He's not a ratepayer, either. Living in lodgings, I expect. Or with some woman he isn't married to."

"All right," said Coulson. "What are you going to do now?"

"Have some lunch, if I'm not too late for it."

"Do that. I've had mine. Now I've got to get back to this *Hoodwink* job. It's working out nicely."

15

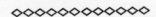

In the preparations for *Exercise Hoodwink,* Chief Inspector Martineau's problems were of a different sort to those of the Metropolitan and county forces. If smuggled diamonds were being transported in the way he had surmised, Granchester, Birmingham, Coventry, and other engineering centers would have to make terminal arrangements. They were at the receiving end.

All the work in connection with *Hoodwink* was in anticipation of one certain event on a certain date. It was a waiting game, and in the meantime the crimes of Granchester's million-and-some people had to be given attention. The night's crime reports of Martineau's division were put on his desk every morning as usual, and all of them were perused. At such times diamonds were usually far from his mind.

October was nearing its end, but the weather was

still unusually fine for that time of year in England. Moreover, it looked like remaining so, and people were happily telling each other that it would shorten the winter. That was all very well, but the nights were long and dark, and a fine, dark night is an encouragement to a person with felonious intent. In consequence, the police were busy with a great many unplanned break-ins, sexual offenses, bag snatchings, and wanton assaults: "small" crimes hard to clear. There were of course bigger crimes also, and Martineau had put himself on call night and day. So it happened that late on a Thursday night he received a telephone call at his home, and the name of Hervey Crube the diamond merchant was mentioned. And at once he was back again among the problems of the illegal disposal of gemstones and toolstones.

Hervey Crube had been waylaid in a fairly busy street as he strolled home from the little inn where he habitually spent his evenings with a few old cronies. Three men walking behind him suddenly pulled scarves over their faces up to the eyes and hustled him into an alley. There, after turning one or two corners he was tied and blindfolded and kept for about an hour in a place which smelled like a repair garage while one of the men went away with his keys. In utter silence the other two waited with him until their accomplice returned. Then his keys were dropped back into his pocket while a small parcel of good gemstones was taken from his waistcoat pocket. After that he was taken back to the place where he had been attacked, and left standing there, blindfolded and with his hands tied behind his back. When at last a passer-by released him he called the police.

Detective Constables Cassidy and Hearn answered

the call. They went with Hervey to his office and found the safe open and empty. Hervey estimated his losses from the safe at fifteen thousand pounds, and he also claimed that the gemstones taken from his pocket had been worth four thousand seven hundred.

Martineau was called at his home. It was after midnight then, but he got out of bed and went down to Headquarters. He listened to Hervey's story. The precise timing and impeccable discipline of the robbery made him think of Dixie Costello. "No talking, no smoking, not an unnecessary move," he said thoughtfully.

He questioned Hervey to satisfy himself as far as possible that the whole business had not been faked for the purpose of claiming insurance, then he realized that if he did not go after Costello's men he would be asked why he had not done so. He put all his available men to the task.

Neither Costello himself nor any of his men was at home in bed. The wife of George Waddington alias Waddy volunteered that they all were at Blackpool, at a coming-out party at some hotel. The party was to celebrate the release from prison of Goosey Bright and Wall Eye Wallace, both valued Costello men.

Blackpool police were informed, and in the morning they located the entire gang at the Cliffs Edge Hotel, and there was abundant evidence that they had spent the previous evening and all the night in Blackpool. It was a perfect alibi.

The alibi made Martineau even more suspicious. It was too pat. He instructed his squad to contact their informers with a view to finding out if Costello had recently recruited new men; men whose membership in the mob was not yet known to the police. He left Costello alone, but in spite of the alibi he rounded up the rest of the mob when they returned to Granchester. He questioned them, but learned nothing of importance. It was one of those duties expected to be futile but intended to show that everything possible had been done.

Informers supplied the names of four new men working for Costello. None of the four had been at the Blackpool party. They were interrogated, and their alibis were suspiciously complete. Martineau realized that unless he received some information about the whereabouts of the stolen property he would not be able to clear the case. He wondered in which of Costello's clubs, gambling shops, or other premises the loot was now hidden. He sighed when he remembered that Costello probably owned businesses about which the police knew nothing. Probably the diamonds had already been channeled away. Could one of the channels have been Mr. Aaron White, who was so reluctant to tell the police when he had been robbed? Was there a link between Costello and White?

At ten minutes before midnight on the Sunday following the day of Hervey Crube's misfortune, the night watchman at Rumbold's Wharf in the Pool of London was leaning on the high window sill of his little office. The window was wide open, and he enjoyed the cool night air even while he polluted it with the reek of a foul old pipe. Below him, but not far below, the river glistened black and oily as the distant shore lights caught its little ripples. It was high water, but there was not much shipping moving in the Lower Pool.

He had been standing there for some minutes when he removed his pipe from his mouth in order to give his whole attention to a phenomenon which was on or under the surface of the water. He was still staring at this when he was invited by the P.L.A. policeman whose duty it was to make contact with him twice a night.

"Phew," said the policeman. "You smoking old rope again, Fred?"

"Thick twist. None better," Fred replied absently, still watching the river.

The policeman came to rest his elbows on the sill. "What you looking at?"

"That light on the water. That cargo boat across there, downriver a bit. There's a sort of glow, nearly amidships."

The policeman looked. "What is it? Phosphorescence?"

Fred had been a deep-water seaman for years of his life. He scoffed. "In London River? Give over!"

"What can it be, then?"

"I dunno. It's slack water all right, but I've never known divers to work in the dark."

"You think it's under the water?"

"It looks so. If it's a diver, there must be summat right seriously wrong with the ship."

At that moment the light vanished. The two men continued to watch. They saw nothing else, and no disturbance of the water where the light had been.

"Funny," the policeman commented. He lit a cigarette, and made a remark about Millwall Football Club. Both men were supporters of the club. They discussed the previous day's match, and the light on the water was forgotten for the time being. Not until the policeman realized that he had smoked his cigarette to a stub did he look at his watch. "Oh, hell," he said. "I'm late for my point, and I haven't had a visit yet."

He departed in haste, and he was ten minutes late

when he reached his conference point. His heart sank when he saw that both his sergeant and the night-duty inspector were waiting for him. Two of them! They were in a right position to make trouble.

He searched his mind for excuses. There was that light on the water. It was a feeble pretext, but it would have to do.

The inspector said: "All right, Moore?" Then he made a performance of looking at his watch.

"Sorry I'm late, sir," Moore replied. "I've been watching a funny sort of light on the river, or underneath it. The watchman at Rumbold's Wharf spotted it."

"So you both had a cup of tea while you watched it?"

"No, sir," was the truthful reply. "No tea."

There was sarcasm in the inspector's voice. "Where was this so-called light?"

"It was close to a freighter on the other bank, just astern of amidships."

"Oh, very nautical. Was it a bright light?"

"No, sir. I daresay you could miss seeing it. But it was there, all right."

"This sounds like a cock-and-bull tale to me. You'd better show me this freighter."

"Yes, sir. This way, sir."

Moore led the other two to a spot directly across the river from the freighter. "There she is, sir."

"But no light on the water."

"No. We saw it go out."

"Did it go out suddenly?"

"Yes, sir. All at once."

"Was there anything else? Any small boats stirring?"

"No, sir. Not a thing."

"Any ideas about the light?"

"No, sir. Divers don't work at night, as a rule."

"What's the ship? Do you know it?"

"No, sir. As you know, I don't get over the other side on this beat."

"Ah, well," said the inspector. "There would probably be a very simple explanation if we knew it." He was turning away, and the sergeant with him.

"Shall I make out a Suspicious Occurrence report, sir?"

"No. I hardly think it is worth it. What is the watchman's name?"

"Fred Hanks."

"Fred Hanks of Rumbold's Wharf. A man of visions. Come along, Sergeant."

After his visitor had left him, Fred Hanks went away from the window in order to make himself a cup of tea. He did not see the small powerboat which crept by in the very shadow of his own wharf. When he did return to the window the boat was upstream, in midstream with lights showing. He watched the lights grow more distant.

"Funny I didn't see that bloke coming up," he told himself, and then he dismissed the matter from his mind.

The inspector's name was Armour, and he walked with the sergeant to the nearest P.L.A. substation. He entered, and the sergeant continued his rounds. In the station he telephoned privately to the night inspector of the Thames River Police at Wapping.

"Look, Charlie," he said. "Something might have happened. I've just received a verbal report, from a man who's a bit on the simple side but no liar. There's a fair-sized freighter moored nearly opposite Rumbold's

Wharf, downriver a bit. She's gray or light blue, with darker boot-topping. A light on her waterline, under the surface probably, was seen by my man and Rumbold's watchman. It sounds to me as if there was a frogman down there with a light. Those people could be making use of other ships besides the you-know-what, couldn't they? I don't have an opposite number on the other side tonight—"

Charlie interrupted. "You want the name of the ship. I'll go myself, and let you know."

"Be careful."

"An unnecessary admonition."

"There may be nothing to it. On the other hand, it may do us a bit of good."

"Right," said Charlie. "I'm on my way."

Half an hour later he called back. "It's the *Uitenhage*," he said. "It's in *Moody's Ocean Ships*. South African Marine Corporation."

"South Africa? Oho! That should be enough to be going on with. Thanks, my lad. Your name will be mentioned."

"I hope so. It all helps in the rat race. Cheerio."

"Cheerio, Charlie."

Inspector Armour called Gravesend for further information about the *Uitenhage*, and was told that its regular run was South Africa to the North Sea ports. He made out his report, and mentioned the names of all concerned. One copy of the report went to his immediate superior, in a sealed envelope. After some thought he sent another copy, also sealed, by hand to Scotland Yard.

There were no officers of high rank at the Yard at one o'clock in the morning. Armour's letter, marked

"Urgent and Confidential," and addressed to the "Officer in Charge," was opened by the inspector on duty in the Back Hall.

After reading the report, this officer also took time for thought. He perceived its possible importance. The diamond-smuggling case was Chief Superintendent Coulson's pigeon. Did he dare wake up Coulson? Did he dare *not* wake up Coulson!

He called the chief superintendent's home number, and was answered. He apologized for the awakening, and read the report. To his relief Coulson said: "You were right to call me. Now get on to Sergeant Horne and tell him I want him down at the Yard right away."

In his office at the Yard, with Horne at his side, Coulson spoke to the A.C. "C" before he began to rouse half the police chiefs in the country. Russell had sleep in his voice when he answered the phone, but he was soon wide awake. When he had heard the report he said: "Yes. We'll have to do it. It'll be a dress rehearsal at any rate." Then he had a second thought and added: "Get Henty's endorsement."

Henty was called. He backed the Assistant Commissioner's decision, and Coulson and Horne became very busy indeed. Chiefs and deputy chiefs of county and big-city police forces were roused by telephone. Coulson's question was: "Are you ready for *Exercise Hoodwink?*" Whether the answer was yes or no he went on: "The Assistant Commissioner 'C' and Mr. Henty of the Home Office earnestly request you to be ready for tomorrow night. That is to say, Monday night."

He reflected that it would be Monday night by the earliest. The London manager of the diamond runners would need a few hours to sort the new consignment. It also occurred to him that there might be no diamonds. The diver could have been staging a dummy run, getting some practice at working in murky Thames water at night. Well, if the smugglers needed some practice, so did the police. *Hoodwink* would be tricky enough even if the weather conditions were ideal. The search for a needle in a haystack could not be more trying than the task of picking out one unknown car from the thousands leaving London for the provinces in the late evening.

16

Monday night was fine and clear, and Jack Mayhew at the wheel of yet another Jaguar had no fears. He had a theory about the use of stolen cars. The police were keen enough in looking out for them, but if they were changed a little and then hidden away for some time, they were well down the list when they emerged. This Jaguar had been put away in a solidly built lockup garage a month ago. Its number plates corresponded with the number on the Road Fund license, which had been stolen from another Jaguar. After this journey, it would be returned to its garage, and would not be brought out again until there was another journey to be made. The car was safe enough, unless it happened to be caught in a police check. Mayhew was not afraid of that. There was a man called Wilmot sitting by his side who was going to make sure that it did not happen.

Half an hour before midnight Mayhew turned left out of Brondesbury Road in Kilburn and took the road to the northwest. Kilburn High Road changed its name as it went along, but it became Watling Street at Edgware and Mayhew knew it as the A5. He followed this road, crossing the beginning of the M1 at Elstree, preferring the older road because the motorway would be well policed.

After Elstree, Wilmot tuned his Xavier radio on to the Hertfordshire police wavelength, and the unemotional routine messages could be clearly heard. There was nothing to worry about. P.C. Jackson reported going off duty to get his supper. P.C. O'Connor was sent to an address in St. Albans to tell somebody that Rosie Hatchett wanted bailing out. Car number 24 was sent to an accident, also at St. Albans.

Then there was a change in the operator's tone. "Calling all cars," he said. "Message four-four-nine. Man answering description of Barry Chivers reported seen on Cricklewood Broadway trying to get a ride north or northwest, at 11:45. F Plan on M1 at Slip End, A5 at Redbourn, A6 at Hatching Green, A405 at Colney Heath, A414 coming out of St. Albans."

"Stop somewhere quick," said Wilmot.

There was not much traffic thereabouts at that time. Mayhew pulled into the side of the road. As the message was repeated Wilmot used a scribble pad with a small light attached, and tried to write down the details.

Both of them knew about Barry Chivers. It had been in all the papers. He had shot two unarmed detectives in Soho, and the police had been hunting him for two days.

"That mug!" said Mayhew with venom. "Idiots like that only make things difficult for other people."

"For honest crooks like us, you mean," said Wilmot

calmly. He had put the Xavier radio down at his feet and was opening a map. "Hold the torch. I need a good light for this job."

He studied the map, finding all the roads on which, presumably, the police were setting up check points.

"I see the game," he said at last. "If Chivers tries to get through to the Midlands they'll get him, and they're blocking him off from the North Road on A405 and A414."

"So what do we do? Turn back and get on to the North Road at Barnet?"

"Maybe. But I see a B road here they didn't bother to cover. It's about three quarters of a mile from here, the other side of Radlett. It seems to trickle through to the A1, just missing London Colney and Colney Heath. We won't need to stop and read the road number. It's the only turning for a mile or two."

"It'll have to cross the A6," said Mayhew, alarmed at the idea.

"Yes, but nowhere near their roadblock. That's quite a way farther north. A place called Hatching Green, the man said."

"All right," said Mayhew. "I'm only the driver." He started the car, and soon they were passing through the quiet little town of Radlett. Beyond the town, at the top of a gentle rise, a signpost pointed eastward.

"Turn off here," said Wilmot. "And then follow your nose."

Mayhew obeyed. As his companion had predicted, they crossed the A6 in safety. B556 was deserted all the way to Colney Heath, and only one car passed them at the crossroads there. Three minutes later they came to the A1. Mayhew turned left, and the car sped almost due north. Safely out of the trap, its occupants listened to yet another repetition of Message 449, and Wilmot patted the Xavier radio with affection.

Message 449, concerning Barry Chivers, was quite false. Chivers had not been seen in Cricklewood, and there were no roadblocks. Later there would be news that the man assumed to have been Chivers had been identified as an ordinary hitchhiker trying to get a ride to Leicester. As part of the exercise, this matter would also be given to the press as a genuine news item.

Though there were no policemen blocking any of the roads mentioned in the message, policemen were vigilant on those roads, though not at the places specified. For instance, days ago an inspector of the Hertfordshire force had pointed out that B556 was a very handy way through from the A5 to the Great North Road. And so, on the night of this almost unexpected "rehearsal," there was a P.C. lying under a hedge at the T junction of A5 and B556.

Because there was radio silence on all things concerning *Hoodwink*—except of course the false messages —the P.C. was equipped with a field telephone which had been run out to his observation post. He also had a ground sheet to lie on, and in order to read number plates not properly illuminated he had a powerful flashlight which had been fitted with a glazed cardboard shade, so that no side flash would be noticeable when he had to use it. He had lain there since ten o'clock, reporting the number and available description of every vehicle which turned aside from the A5 at that spot. He did not know the times of the false messages, or even that there were any, but an inspector at the police station in Radlett was fully informed, and when he was told that Jaguar XYL 4342 had turned aside, he knew that the Chivers message had been sent out five minutes before. He put down XYL 4342 on a special list.

The policeman watching B556 was only one of hundreds stationed at selected turning points on all roads out of London, and later that night there would be hundreds more at turning points still farther afield. Also, Message 449 was only one of a number of false messages being sent out on the wave lengths of county police forces. Every one was calculated to cause a change of direction by any unauthorized listener anxious to avoid the police.

The B556 constable had reported 29 cars turning to take that byway since ten o'clock. It was expected that most of these would be owned by local people, and in fact observers farther along reported only seven of them emerging on to the A1 and two turning up in St. Albans, apparently having detoured to drop friends at their homes. All the others had, seemingly, stopped at London Colney or Colney Heath, or in the country round about, and no doubt their owners would be putting them away for the night.

Of the seven that reached the A1, two turned aside at Hatfield and four went into Welwyn. There were many vehicles speeding north along the A1 beyond Welwyn, but only one of them had joined the road after being reported as crossing from another arterial road by a B/road. It was the dark-colored Jaguar, XYL 4342. It was now reported as SV for Special Vigilance.

Other cars on other roads were being written down SV. Those which did not reach a destination between one observation point and another would eventually be tested again with false news, to see if any would again turn aside. Eventually, one car would clearly identify itself by its own movements. That car would receive a welcome at the journey's end, but it was hoped that its occupants would not notice the welcoming committee.

At Scotland Yard, Coulson with a battery of telephones was trying to keep track of those "turners" which had been marked SV. There were well-trained policewomen at the phones, also two working at a big map and two running liaison between telephonists and mappers. Like the men of subordinate ranks manning observation posts on the roads, these girls knew only that this was an exercise designed to pick out a suspect car through its movements. No doubt they would assume that the suspect car was manned by police officers behaving like crooks on the run. This was a practice game, or a sort of experiment in tactics, but they were prevented from being lighthearted about it by the presence of the A.C. "C" himself. He was merely a spectator, but it was obvious to all that he was taking the keenest interest in everything.

Naturally in an exercise so widespread there were a few mishaps and mistakes. Cars were "lost," seeming to have dropped out of sight by accident or by their drivers' intent. In these cases one of Martineau's safeguards came into operation. There were two policemen beside a telephone in every city, borough, and county licensing office in the country. When observers lost trace of a car its local registration was determined by its serial letters, and the local office was informed. The number was checked for ownership, and the owner was sought at his address. Eventually, as the night wore on, every one of these few "lost" cars was found, either in its owner's garage or standing outside his house.

At 12:45, after a hectic ninety minutes, every "turner" except one had been cleared of suspicion and eliminated from the exercise, and only two "lost" cars were still being sought, both of these from licensing offices in the home counties.

While he waited for news of these two Coulson kept track of the one "turner" which had not yet reached a destination. This was Jaguar XYL 4342, going north on the A1 and checked past Peterborough and Stamford. He was beginning to have great hopes of the Jaguar, and he decided that it had traveled far enough without interruption. He thought that a second test message could be put out without arousing suspicion. He spoke to the Lincolnshire County police.

"There's a good one coming your way," he said. "Jaguar XYL 4342. Be careful with it. I think it might be *the* car."

"It bypassed Stamford."

"Yes. I think soon after Grantham will be the time, to turn it at Newark or thereabouts. Have you a good story?"

"Yes. Two men escaped from Brinstall, near here. It's a criminal mental hospital. We'll give a preliminary message, now, that it's thought they will be heading for Lincoln or Tuxford where their respective homes are. Later, we'll give a second message about check points, just after Grantham."

"Fine. What about Nottingham? Will you arrange for them to broadcast the second message three or four minutes after you?"

"Yes. We'll do that."

"Good. I hope to hear from you."

17

Mayhew kept the Jaguar to a steady 65 miles an hour to avoid the notice of policemen. But as the car swept northward he became concerned about direction.

"We're off our road," he said. "It'll throw us late."

"Not so much," Wilmot told him. "We're bearing slightly westward. We can leave this road just east of Worksop and make straight for Sheffield. Then from Sheffield straight over the moors. There'll be no coppers up there, and I know the road."

"As you say," said Mayhew, partly satisfied. "Hello, Grantham coming up."

At the moment something else came up. It was Message 193, from Lincoln. "Smith and Halford, escaped Brinstall Mental Hospital, thought to be heading for Tuxford or Lincoln, where their homes are."

"Different accent they have up here," Mayhew commented. "No roadblocks, at any rate."

"Maybe not, but I don't like it," the other man said. "Tuxford is right in our path. The coppers'll be on the lookout around there. We'd better make for Mansfield. I think it'll actually be a more direct way, though I don't know it."

"Where will we turn for Mansfield?"

"Newark, I think. I'll look."

But he did not immediately look at the map. Lincoln spoke again: "Message 194. Re Smith and Halford. F Plan on A1 at North Muskham, and at North Hykeham on A46."

Wilmot scribbled on his pad. "I'll have to look."

"Can't stop here," said Mayhew.

"I'll manage," he was told.

He did manage, finding the roads and the two tiny places mentioned.

"Yes," he said. "They're blocking off Lincoln and Tuxford. They're both north of Newark. At Newark we take the A617."

They heard Message 194 repeated as they approached Newark, and somehow Mayhew managed to miss the bypass. He had to drive down into the town. There he had a minute or two of indecision, with Wilmot insisting that Mansfield *must* be a left turn, and then he found the road.

The Jaguar's divergence from the Great North Road, and the turn in Newark were both observed and reported, and this development led to a discussion in Nottingham.

"We don't want to assume too much about these fellows," a chief superintendent said. "They turned once near London and came north. Nobody knows what part of London they came from, so the turn could have been made for an innocent reason. Now we don't know where they're going. They could have turned quite innocently at Newark, making for Sheffield via Mansfield. I know it isn't the most direct road, but how do we know the passenger isn't going to get off somewhere along that road? That is, assuming it's on an innocent errand."

"I'm not very good at assuming innocence," an assistant chief said. "We have the men out, and it's the only suspect car which has got so far, so we might as well watch it through."

"But why not make sure of it?" the other man persisted. "An addition to that Brinstall message wouldn't raise any suspicion."

"You mean, turn them at Mansfield?"

"Yes. Block them from both Chesterfield and Worksop, and see what happens."

"We could try it," said the assistant reluctantly.

The map was consulted, and a message went out. It was to the effect that a lorry driver making directly for Sheffield on the A616 had reported seeing two men climb down, apparently from the top of his load, when he stopped at a crossing in Cuckney. They had run off along the Chesterfield road. It was thought that they might be Smith and Halford. Special vigilance by all patrols was requested on the roads from east and southeast into Chesterfield.

"Stop the car," Wilmot said. "Those two loonies are going to get us into trouble if we're not careful."

He looked at his map, and discovered the A616 was a more direct route from Newark to Sheffield than the Mansfield road. Reading the map in the moving car on the approach to Newark, he had failed to observe this road. He did not mention the oversight to Mayhew.

"We'll have to turn aside in Mansfield," he said. "There seems to be only one road we can go: A615 to a place called Alfreton. Oy! Wait a minute. There's a road directly through from Alfreton to the A6 at Matlock."

"And the A6 will take us right to Granchester," said Mayhew. "Thank Christ for that."

In the center of Mansfield there was five minutes of blind circling, with Mayhew cursing under his breath, around apparently deserted one-way streets and squares. But A615 was found at last, and the Jaguar fled west and slightly south to Alfreton. This change of direction was observed and reported, and two senior officers in Nottingham were convinced that the exercise had been a success: the Jaguar had been picked out from thousands leaving London, and it was undoubtedly on an unlawful errand of some kind. Moreover, it was obviously equipped with the means of picking up police messages.

At half past three in the morning Mayhew and Wilmot reached Alfreton, and found that little town even harder asleep than Mansfield. But there were no one-way streets. They took only one turning, and then at a crossing Wilmot's torch picked out "Matlock" on a sign. They took this road, and in Matlock they turned northwest along the A6.

The police checked them all the way in to Granchester, a distance of some 45 miles. They were not aware of observation and they were not troubled again. The police were sure of them now, and only wished to note their destination.

Granchester waited quietly for Jaguar XYL 4342. Detective Chief Inspector Martineau had been allowed to take charge of the reception details, because he had

devised them. When he learned that the car had taken
the A6 at Matlock, he assumed that it was making for
either Liverpool or Granchester. When the car was still
on the A6 after Buxton, he ruled out Liverpool and
decided that entry into Granchester would almost certainly be along the road from Stockport. He gave this
news by telephone to men who waited on the streets.

There was a policeman in plain clothes concealed
near every public and police telephone in the entire
police district. All the police telephones had been origi-
nally sited near to crossroads, so that the network of
men on foot covered the city quite effectively.

There was radio silence for the plain police cars
which were out, except for routine messages not concerned with *Exercise Hoodwink,* and certain code messages which sounded like routine and meant something
else entirely. Each car had been allotted an area, or
beat, and would go into action and search the streets
only on reception of a code message which would inform their drivers that the observers on foot had "lost"
the Jaguar. To alert them to the fact that this car was
imminently due to arrive there was a message instruct-
ing the crew of car AP9 to go to Wales Road, where a
smell of burning had been reported near to McCrea's
cotton warehouse.

As it happened, the cars were not needed. Checked
and reported on all the way, Jaguar XYL 4342 entered
Granchester and sped along apparently deserted main
streets straight into the heart of the city. It was finally
observed by a young P.C. in plain clothes who was
standing in a deep, dark shop entrance near the crossing
of Lacy Street and Crossley Street. He saw the Jaguar
go over the crossing and turn to go along a quiet little
street which ran between the main streets of Bishopsgate and Crossley Street. When the car disappeared, he

sprinted the fifty yards to the corner and was in time to see the car stationary, with two men getting out of it. One of the men appeared to lean into the back of the car and be busy for a moment, then he turned and went with his companion to the back door of the Tahiti Club. The door of the club opened, and closed silently when they had entered.

The P.C.'s name was Norton, and he thought that a place like the Tahiti Club was a strange choice as the terminal of a police exercise, but his instructions were clear. He hurried to the nearby telephone and spoke to Headquarters.

At that time there was no less a person than Inspector Pearson of the C.I.D. on the HQ switchboard. Pearson heard the message, and asked: "You're sure of the number?"

"Yes, sir. XYL 4342. I saw it clearly by the crossing light as it passed me."

"Very well. Come in here to me at once, and don't speak to a soul on the way."

Norton may have had reason to be surprised by this abrupt order, but he simply said, "Yes, sir," and replaced the receiver.

Pearson handed over the switchboard to the regular operator. He caught Martineau's eye as he rose from his seat. The two men left the extension of the front office which was A Division's Information Room, and went into the corridor which led to the C.I.D.

"The Jag is in Bowyer Street, at the back door of the Tahiti Club," Pearson said in a low voice. "Two men left the car and went into the club."

"Who spotted it?"

"Two-one-eight Norton, D Division. I told him to come in, and keep his mouth shut."

"Right. We'll call off the cars, but not the men on the phone boxes. You'll have to talk to Norton when he comes in. I'll nip out to Bowyer Street."

He returned to the Information Room, and from there a message informed car AP9 that the fire in Wales Road was nothing more than some smoldering rubbish in a dustbin. This was the signal which withdrew the C.I.D. cars from the exercise. Then Martineau went out to the yard where his own middle-aged Jaguar was parked and drove to a quiet street off Lacy Street. He left the car there and walked to the end of Bowyer Street. The suspect Jaguar was still outside the Tahiti Club.

Inspector Pearson was waiting for P.C. Norton when he walked into A Division station. He did not speak, but led the way into his own office in the C.I.D. His expression was stern, but he relaxed when he saw that Norton was of a type who would not be impressed by histrionics.

"Sit down," he said. "You may have done yourself a bit of good this morning. But you are also in possession of dangerous knowledge."

"You mean the club, sir?"

"Yes. This exercise has *not* been a dummy run. It's a real job, and it is top secret. It's so important that Whitehall is watching it. So you will have to remain silent—absolutely silent—about seeing the car at that club. Not a word to anyone at all. Have you passed for sergeant?"

"Yes, sir."

"Well, there you are. You've done yourself a good turn, but not if you open your mouth to anybody."

Mention of Whitehall had not changed Norton's expression. He said: "Naturally I won't breathe a word."

For a moment Pearson stared steadily at this unusually self-possessed young officer, then he opened a drawer of his desk. In the drawer he kept report forms of various kinds. He brought out a "plain" form and a manila envelope. He said: "Stay in this room to write your report. Put it in this envelope and seal it, and address it to Chief Superintendent Clay. Mark it 'Confidential,' then bring it to me personally. If I'm not around, give it to the duty inspector. Nobody beneath the rank of inspector must see it."

"Very good, sir," said Police Constable Norton.

The Jaguar waited behind the Tahiti Club for thirty-five minutes, then two men emerged from the club and drove away. The car went round into Bishopsgate and then into Lacy Street, and headed back the way it had come. Martineau kept out of sight and let it go, and remained to watch the club. He waited only fifteen minutes longer, and then he saw André Vidor and that red-haired girl of his walk across Lacy Street at Bishopsgate, as if they had emerged from the front door of the club. Neither of them was carrying a bag or a parcel, and the girl did not even have a handbag.

Vidor was the manager of the Tahiti Club. He was also the nominal owner, but Martineau suspected that the real owner was Dixie Costello.

He did not follow the couple. The streets were too quiet for such an operation to be safe.

Jaguar XYL 4342 was checked on its return journey, in case there might be a second delivery in the Birmingham area. This seemed possible when it took the Chester Road, and then the M6 after passing through Altrincham. Tired men saw it go by, and made their last calls and went off duty with a fervent hope that

Exercise Hoodwink was not going to become a regular thing.

Birmingham remained a possibility until the Jaguar reached the crossing of the A5 at Hatherton, and turned left. The A5 took it straight across country from motorway to motorway, bringing it to the M1 east of Rugby. On the M1 to its end, and then again on the A5, it was driven straight to London.

In London's midmorning traffic it was not difficult to trail the car. It was picked up at Uxbridge and followed by first one plain police vehicle and then another to Hammersmith, where it was driven into an open yard made by a square formation of concrete lockup garages. After a few minutes Mayhew and Wilmot emerged from the yard in a Mini Cooper which was known to be Mayhew's own car. Wilmot alighted from the Mini in Walham Green and was seen to enter a house there. Mayhew went on his way, and eventually turned along a street near the shabbier end of the King's Road. He entered a house there, and left his little car at the curb.

18

André Vidor and the red-haired girl had appeared in Granchester about a year before, and they had seemed to strike up a friendship with Dixie Costello almost at once. At least they were seen with him a great deal, and this was what made Martineau notice them. Any associate of Costello was worth his notice.

A few months later the Tahiti Club came into being, and under the new Granchester bylaw concerning clubs, Vidor's record was checked. He had a South African passport, and no police record in either Britain or South Africa. After the opening of the club he was seen less often with Costello, and it was assumed that his new job as club manager was keeping him busy. And apparently he was a good manager. The club seemed to be doing well. Recently he had moved with the red-

140

head to a better address, and he had acquired a new Rover car, probably on hire purchase.

That was as much as Martineau had felt that he needed to know about Vidor, until the Tahiti Club became important as a terminal of *Exercise Hoodwink*. That changed everything. He still could not approach Vidor, and he also decided on safety grounds that it would be unwise to put an undercover man into the club, but there were things he wanted to know.

It occurred to him that Vidor might be known to Interpol, but he did not approach that organization directly. He asked Coulson of the Yard to do it. Coulson was delighted with what he called "the touchdown" in Granchester, and he readily promised his assistance.

At Coulson's request, Interpol clicked into action. Through its contacts it very soon produced the information that Vidor had no police record under his own name anywhere in the non-Communist world. Nevertheless, he was known to Interpol. This knowledge harked back to the palmy days of Tangier, when it was an international free port and a nest of money manipulators, wanted criminals, and smugglers. In Tangier Vidor had not bothered to conceal his activities as a smuggler, running contraband to Spain, Italy, and France. He had also been known as a first-rate seaman, and this circumstance was mentioned to the South African police. They discovered that an André Vidor had been cashiered from the South African Navy for a check offense. This hiatus in his career had occurred a year or so before his appearance in Tangier.

Having waited anxiously for information of any kind, Lieutenant Kropp and his colleagues followed up the Vidor news with energy, but they worked quietly. First, there was André's birth certificate, and the marriage certificate of his parents. South African-born John Vidor had married French-born Annette Dubose in 1916. They had had four sons, Pierre, Raoul, Didier, and André. John and Annette had been dead for some years, but there was no death certificate bearing the name of any of the sons. Not one of the four brothers had a criminal record, but search in Marriage brought the information that Raoul Vidor had married Irma Couperus in 1947, and the investigation turned on families with that surname. Eventually Irma Vidor was found. She was a grass widow with two grown-up daughters. Her husband Raoul had deserted her in 1953, and she had been too proud to have the police seek him for failing to maintain her and the children. She had no idea what happened to him but she did have some wedding photographs. The police were allowed to make copies of Raoul's picture. They were given an estimate of his height and build, and they were told of his habits, likes, and dislikes.

No information about brothers Pierre and Didier was turned up, but the search for Raoul began in earnest. A few days later a policeman in Windhoek recognized the man in the wedding picture as one Ronald Vincent, whom he had once met while on annual leave in Swakopmund. Vincent, he believed, had been a personnel officer for the Diamond Syndicate in South-West Africa.

"Ronald Vincent" was quickly located, still working for the Syndicate. The Syndicate's undercover security men, highly skilled in this sort of investigation, closed in unobtrusively on Raoul Vidor alias Vincent, spotting his contacts one by one, but were content to remain undercover until matters in England came to a head.

In England the inquiries about André Vidor's red-haired paramour remained local in character. Martineau had a feeling that he had seen her before, but years ago. Well, there was one P.C. on the force who was in the Tahiti Club secret. Martineau had a word with Chief Superintendent Clay about this P.C. Norton, and Clay had the man seconded to C.I.D. duties in A Division.

Martineau looked at Norton's personal file, and whistled. The young man was the sort of officer for whom police pundits had been crying out. He was a graduate with honors in law, and the university was Oxford, no less. While his qualifications might mean rapid promotion for him in a few years' time, it had made no difference to his treatment as a recruit. He had to go through the mill, do the drudgery, and gain practical experience.

He appeared before Martineau in plain clothes. He was a fine boy, quite big enough for his job. He was handsome, and his face showed that intangible quality which people call breeding. This stamp of upbringing and schooling made Martineau realize that he was extremely unlikely to be taken for a policeman. Indeed, it was a matter of surprise to the chief inspector that a man with Norton's opportunities ever had become a policeman. However, here he was, looking like an ideal undercover man.

"Sit down, Norton," he said. "You're the only P.C. in this force who knows about the Tahiti Club, so we may as well use you on the job. Are you willing, or would you sooner go back on the beat?"

"I'm quite willing, sir."

"Very good. A man called Vidor runs the Tahiti, and Interpol has given us some help with him. But he lives with a red-haired girl, and Interpol can't help us with her because we don't know her name. Not even her first name. It is going to be your job to find out. And this business is so ticklish that you'll have to find out without asking. Not one single question must you ask."

"I listen, sir."

"You listen without seeming to listen. The Lacy Arms and the Northland Hotel are favorite spots with Vidor. You'll spend a lunchtime hour in the bars of those places. I'll give you descriptions of Vidor and the girl, so that together you won't mistake them. They're both exceptionally good-looking. I want you to try to hear what her friends call her. Just the first name. That will have to do for a start."

Norton memorized the descriptions and went on his errand, and twenty minutes in the same bar as Vidor and the girl was all he needed.

"I heard someone call the woman Donna, sir," he reported to Martineau.

"Donna. It might be short for something. But we'll see what we can do with it. I have an idea that she's a local girl, and she might have some form. I want you to go through all the local record cards on women, starting with A. Make a note of all Donnas, Dianas, and similar names. It will be a dreary job, but you can take as much time as you like. If the clerk in C.R.O. gets nosy, refer him to me."

That conversation occurred at two o'clock in the afternoon. At half past four Norton returned with a record card. "I thought you might like to see this one, sir," he said.

Martineau took the card and read aloud: "Harlan, Donna. 41 Blaydon Street, Churlham. Born 1939. Height five feet four inches. Hair dark red or auburn, eyes light brown, medium build, no distinguishing marks. Larceny servant, July 18, 1955. One year's probation."

He looked up and nodded his approval. "She'll be about twenty-seven now, so the year of birth is right. In

1955 she'd be about sixteen, and she's grown an inch since then. It looks as if this could be the girl. Go and see if you can find the report."

Norton went, and returned with a crime report dated July 18, 1955. The report and the attached statements gave Martineau the story. Donna Harlan, recently out of school and working in a small dress shop, had been sent by her employer to the bank, to get change for three five-pound notes. In an hour she had not returned, and the dressmaker telephoned the bank. She learned that Donna had indeed called at the bank, where she was known, but instead of getting the large and small silver required she had asked for fifteen one-pound notes. The dressmaker called the police.

A Detective Constable Parry, since retired, went at once to see the woman. It was a damp morning, and he was told that Donna had been wearing a belted raincoat and a beret, thus still looking rather like a school-girl.

"What sort of a girl is she?" he asked. "Fond of the lads?"

"I don't know what she does when she isn't working," the woman replied. "I do know she's screen-struck. She doesn't seem to have anything else in her head."

So Parry at once phoned Passenger Inquiries at the South Midland Station, and learned that a nonstop Pullman train had departed for London only ten minutes before. He went to the station and interviewed the clerk in Pullman Reservations. He remembered the "school-girl."

"Just a kid, very pretty," he said. "Red hair and sort of tan-colored eyes. Raincoat and beret. I thought she looked nearly too young to be traveling on her own."

That made things easy for Parry. He made another phone call, and as a result the runaway girl was met at

Euston Station by two policewomen. She still had twelve pounds in her possession, and she told the policewomen that she had intended to try to get work in a film studio.

One year's probation had been her punishment for that escapade, and there was nothing further on her record.

"She's been a good girl since then," Norton ventured to remark.

"Yes, or else she's been more careful."

"Churlham. That looks like a rough neighborhood to me."

"Blaydon Street isn't too bad. It's on the Lea Park side of Churlham. What you might call respectable working class. Let's see what the Burgess Roll says."

According to the Burgess Roll, another family now lived at 41 Blaydon Street, but an earlier edition placed the Harlan family there. Apparently someone had consulted that edition in 1955. There was a marginal note in pencil: "Son *Roger* Harlan. Donna half sister."

"That would be Parry," Martineau commented. "He seemed to think that Roger was worth somebody's attention. All right, now we'll turn up Roger Harlan."

Again Norton went to look at record cards, and returned with the one required.

"Plenty of form, sir," he announced. "But mainly juvenile."

The card announced that Roger had been born in 1928, which made him eleven years older than Donna. Apparently he had been a very bad boy from twelve to eighteen: petty larceny mainly, but no fewer than three housebreaking charges. These latter had landed him in a Borstal Institution, and since then there was only one offense marked against him, in 1957. And, considering the nature of his earlier crimes, this last one seemed out of character. He had been charged with obtaining credit without declaring himself an undischarged bankrupt. And in spite of his earlier bad record, he had escaped with three years' probation.

"That sounds like extenuating circumstances," Martineau remarked. "Go and see if you can find the reports. And I want the Borstal record."

Norton departed, and returned. Notes about the Borstal record were attached to the "credit while undischarged" file. Apparently Roger had been one young criminal who had benefited from Borstal reform. He had been taught engineering—the trade to which he had been apprenticed—and according to the record he had worked and studied hard. Also his general conduct had been good. His leaving certificate declared that he was quite competent as both a fitter and a toolmaker.

The Borstal report was followed by a letter from the machine-tool maker who had employed Roger from 1949 to 1954. It stated that he had been a satisfactory workman.

"He was playing it straight, all right," said Martineau, slightly surprised.

Further information was now found; the statement of the arresting officer, which had been read to the court in the interests of fair play. The statement explained that in 1955 Roger had set up in business for himself, in a lockup garage with secondhand machine tools. Things had not gone well for him. His savings had melted away, and in less than two years he had been bankrupted, having debts of £520 and assets which brought in £90.

He had gone back to work for an employer, but every month he had paid through an accountant twenty pounds, with the intention of eventually having the bankruptcy order rescinded.

"Good for him," Martineau murmured as he read.

Apparently Roger was still determined to go into

business for himself, because early in 1957 he had been tempted by the opportunity to rent some ideal premises on very favorable terms. He saw it as a chance of a lifetime. He rented the premises and bought tools on credit. Though they were not new, their price was £125. This time he did fairly well, but not well enough to have saved that amount of money in three months. He offered to pay part of what he owed, but his creditor had heard something about him. And apparently he was a vindictive man. Failing to get the entire amount owing, he reported the matter to the police.

But the statement had a happy ending. A gentleman who had wished to remain anonymous had become interested in Roger's case. It had been his intention to pay all the debts and have the bankruptcy order rescinded, and it was to be supposed that he had done this. Nevertheless, Roger had been put on probation.

At the end of his reading Martineau sat in thought. Then he reached for the telephone book. A Roger Harlan was listed at an address in Highfield, Granchester. And the next entry was: "Harlan, Roger Ltd., Century Engineering Works, Mount Street, Granchester."

So Roger was still in business, backed no doubt by his Good Samaritan. Martineau pondered who that might be.

Then suddenly he sat bolt upright, staring at Norton but not seeing him. He remembered now where he had seen the Harlan girl. He calculated. In 1957 she would be about eighteen, just the right age. She was the right type, red-haired, tallish, good figure. Yes, he remembered now. About that time she had been Costello's current popsie. And it was just possible that she had persuaded him to help her half brother. Did Costello now have a substantial share in a small engineering firm? That was something which might never be discovered.

But André Vidor was receiving diamonds, and his sweetheart's brother had an engineering shop. And no doubt he would be able to make diamond-tipped tools. It was, to say the least, an interesting situation.

"We'd better be sure we're on to the right girl," Martineau said. He spoke on the internal line to the assistant chief clerk, who was the unpaid local agent of Police Mutual Insurance.

"Ben," he said, "does Tom Parry still come in to pay his subs?"

"Sure. He still has a whole life policy. I see him once every three months."

"What's he doing?"

"A real soft job. Security, Granchester Cotton."

"Day or night?"

"Day. He's in charge. Has a staff."

"Thanks, Ben."

Martineau looked up a number and dialed, and eventually spoke to ex-Constable Parry.

"Harry Martineau here," he said. "How are you?"

"Cushy. A real job. What do you want to know?"

"Cast your mind back ten years. A young girl called Harlan, who ran off to London with some cash."

"I remember. Nice auburn hair she had."

"She still has, but I want to be sure of her. Would you take a look at her and just say yes or no?"

"If it can be managed."

"On your day off, maybe. I'm sending a lad called Norton to see you, and you can fix it up with him. He'll pay for the beer."

"I should hope so. When is he coming?"

"Now," said Martineau.

19

The *Ismailbaksh* was a day late when she sailed into
the Thames Estuary. Her arrival was checked by the
Port of London Authority at Gravesend, and when she
exchanged her estuary pilot for a river pilot the captain
was told that his mooring was Greenwich Buoys. From
there, in deep water, she would discharge castor seed
into lighters.

The Buoys had been suggested by the police because
there were moored lighters nearby on both sides of the
river, and already their observers were hidden on the
lighters. Each team had a telephone and two "magic
eye" cameras. These could take a picture in darkness
with an infrared light which glowed no brighter than
a cigarette end for a very small fraction of a second.
The camera experts of the Metropolitan Police were
quite confident that they would get some good pictures.

It was assumed that the ship's arrival had been observed by someone besides the P.L.A., and watchers by the river were told to look out for a powerboat of some kind which would now be used to locate the mooring. This boat was expected early on the scene, because of the possibility that the ship might go into a dock, and the dock would have to be known.

There was not much traffic coming down the river against the flowing tide, and a smart little cabin cruiser called the *Dutch Girl* was one vessel which came under suspicious scrutiny. In spite of the tide she must have come downstream at speed, because she met the *Ismailbaksh* beyond Erith. Her crew of two barely glanced at the freighter as they passed.

But the *Dutch Girl* turned before Greenhithe and followed the bigger boat at a distance too great for her to be noticed by anyone but the watching police. She passed the *Ismailbaksh* again as that ship moored at Greenwich, and went on upstream. She was not followed, because she was known to the river police. Her regular mooring was near the marine service station below Kew Railway Bridge. She was marked down for special attention. That afternoon she was discreetly located at her mooring, and as discreetly watched. According to *Lloyd's Register* she was owned by one Hector Linslade, of Belsize Park. Linslade's house also was put under observation.

At Scotland Yard Coulson was convinced that a diver would visit the *Ismailbaksh* that same night, because her position seemed to be ideal for him, and also because it would be reasonable for him to think that she might be moved to a dock after part of her cargo had been discharged. Soon after dark the police observers took up their posts, ashore and afloat, at selected points on and beside the river from Greenwich up to Kew.

There were so many C.I.D. men engaged on these and other special duties that "tailing" details had to be withdrawn for one day.

The fine weather persisted. The night was starlit, with no mist and very little wind. At eight o'clock a taxi stopped in Belsize Park, and the man assumed to be Hector Linslade emerged from his house with a woman who could have been his wife. Both were in evening dress, and the taxi took them to the Savoy, which they entered. The hotel was watched. Linslade and his wife did not come out until after eleven o'clock, in the company of friends, and the whole party decorously merry. Cabs were called, and the Linslades were driven home. They went indoors, and did not emerge until morning. Mr. Linslade had an alibi. The police guessed—correctly, as it turned out—that someone was using his boat without his knowledge or permission.

At midnight Kew was quiet, but two local constables of F Division lying flat near the railway bridge saw a man move from behind the marine service station and make his way down to the river. He was a big rangy fellow and one of the officers thought—though he could not be sure—that he knew the man and that he used to be employed at the service station. He stopped at a spot where he was not likely to be seen by a passer-by, and became busy with something he had been carrying. Eventually the policemen perceived that he was inflating a rubber dinghy. While they watched, they heard a car approach and stop somewhere on the other side of the service station. A minute later two more men appeared, also burdened with some sort of equipment. They joined the man at the waterside and all three got into the dinghy. They paddled out to the *Dutch Girl* and boarded her, and pulled the dinghy aboard too.

Two minutes later the *Dutch Girl* began to move

downstream without lights. Her lights did not appear until she was well away from the moorings. One of the watchers on the bridge went to a telephone.

This time the cabin cruiser did not hurry on her fourteen-mile journey. It was after half past one when she cruised down in midstream toward the *Ismailbaksh*. In the darkness she was not identifiable by those who watched her, but she had been checked and timed all the way from Kew, and she was expected. Furthermore, the actions of her crew identified her. They doused their lights three hundred yards upstream from the freighter. The *Dutch Girl* slowed and appeared to drift. Though it was slack water between full flow and ebb of the tide, the boat's drift showed that there was enough current to carry her frogman down to the starboard side of the moored ship.

One watcher thought he saw the frogman slip over the *Dutch Girl's* gunwale into the water, then still without lights the boat crept down past the ship. It stopped in shadow beside the lighters moored a little way downstream, but not far from the stern of the *Ismailbaksh* on the port side. A police observer with an infrared camera was on a lighter less than five yards away from it, peering at it from under the edge of a tarpaulin cover.

Presently the watchers on the lighters across the river saw the eerie reflection of the frogman's light as he worked. They timed him: twelve minutes. The light went out, and then it became apparent that someone on the *Dutch Girl* had also been timing him. Her lights showed, so that he could mark her position as he came round the stern of the *Ismailbaksh* and swim down to her on the current.

He came, and was taken aboard, and the man with the camera got his pictures; all three of the crew including the frogman without his mask. The glow of his infrared bulb was not noticed, each tiny flash being so brief that it had vanished before a human eye could move to locate it.

The *Dutch Girl* moved out to midstream and then went upriver with her lights showing. That part of *Exercise Hoodwink* was over.

At ten minutes to two a uniformed policeman on his beat reached the corner where Flood Street joins Cheyne Walk beside the Chelsea Embankment. Pausing there, he looked past the beginning of the long, narrow shrubbery which divides the Walk from the Embankment, and saw a man leaning on the elbow-high river wall. There was nothing in the man's attitude to indicate that he contemplated suicide, and furthermore the P.C. decided that it was his car which stood on the Cheyne Walk side of the shrubbery, at the end of the long line of residents' parked cars.

"Watching the river and getting a breath of air," he assumed. "Can't sleep, maybe."

The waiting car had not been there when he had passed an hour ago, and also it was the only car in the line showing lights. He was about to move forward when he noticed that two men were sitting in the car. That made a great deal of difference to the situation. It looked suspicious, and he had been told to report any out of the ordinary occurrence on or near the river that night.

From where he stood, he did not think that the man at the wheel of the car could see him in the driver's mirror, and neither man had looked around. The rear light was bright enough for him to read the number plate. He stepped back round the corner, and made a note of the number. Then he went away, to the nearest telephone. Five minutes after he had made his call an inspector and a sergeant of the C.I.D. were on their way to his assistance, in a plain Humber car.

The inspector knew that the *Dutch Girl* was now well on her way back from Greenwich. He also realized that he would not be able to see the river from anywhere near Cheyne Walk without showing himself to the man who leaned on the wall.

He said to the sergeant: "I'll drop you at the top of Flood Street and you can walk down to the corner. I'll take the car round to Chelsea Bridge and join you later."

When the inspector reached the bridge, a good six hundred yards away from Cheyne Walk, he left his car and he also watched the river. Minutes passed, and then a cabin cruiser came under Victoria Railway Bridge. It was in midstream, showing lights, and it was the only vessel in sight. Quite probably it was the only one moving on the Thames above dockland so late at night.

In concealment near the bridge, the inspector watched the boat pass, and then change direction slightly, heading toward the Chelsea side. He knew then what might happen, and he ran to his car. He was in Flood Street before the cabin cruiser could possibly have come near to Cheyne Walk, and he stopped his engine and silently coasted the last hundred yards to the corner.

The P.C. and the C.I.D. sergeant were still there. He drew them back, and lay flat on the ground, to peep round the corner from as far as possible below normal eye level. He saw that the man beside the river was no longer leaning on the wall. He was standing erect, looking downstream. Presently he looked both ways along the Embankment and, briefly, at the bushes behind him. Then he returned his gaze to the river.

Very soon his attitude showed that the *Dutch Girl*

was quite near. And a voice, seemingly from the river, called softly: "Catchee?"

The man on the bank made some reply, and then he lunged to catch something as it came flying over the wall. It looked like a bag, about the size of a briefcase. He caught it deftly, then hurried to the waiting car. A door slammed, the engine roared, and the car sped away along Cheyne Walk. It turned up Oakley Street toward the King's Road.

Perhaps the inspector ought to have allowed his young sergeant to drive the police Humber. When he reached the King's Road there was no sign of any other car. He crossed, and made for the Fulham Road, but when he reached it he turned in the wrong direction. For the moment the suspect car was lost.

There was of course radio silence on all matters relating to the night's operation, but C.I.D. and Flying Squad cars were waiting near telephone boxes at key points all over London. A precautionary message about a medium-sized fawn-colored car YBC 8291 had gone out soon after the Chelsea P.C. had made his first phone call. His second call, to the effect that something had been thrown ashore and collected by the men now in YBC 8291, caused a second and more urgent message to be sent out.

YBC 8291 was seen at Marble Arch and identified as an Austin 1800. It went along Oxford Street and turned to go along Portman Street, and fled almost due north toward Swiss Cottage.

The police car which now followed it was manned by two young detective constables. Bearing in mind that he must avoid notice, the man at the wheel was driving without lights. Also, since his own car and the

Austin were the only vehicles on that road, he had to remain a long way in the rear.

He lost sight of the distant rear light at the bend near Lord's Cricket Ground, but saw it again on long, straight Wellington Road. It again disappeared at a bend, but was still in sight when he rounded it into Finchley Road. Then at Swiss Cottage it disappeared abruptly. He realized that to vanish in that manner the Austin must have turned sharp left into Belsize Road, a change of direction which looked uncommonly like evasive action.

Down the steep hill of Belsize Road the police car went in pursuit. This road was just as deserted as the other one had been, and at the bottom of the hill the Austin's rear light came into sight again, away on the straight stretch to Kilburn. A few seconds later it disappeared again.

"He turned right," said Detective Constable Bromley, in the passenger seat.

The driver, whose name was Wood, nodded in the darkness of the car. He was driving at top speed now, knowing that he would have to get nearer to the Austin or lose it. He turned right at Abbey Road and followed it round into Quex Road, and at Kilburn High Road he stopped.

The Kilburn Road, one of the roots of the Great North Road, was not deserted. There was sparse traffic, and away to the right were two sets of retreating taillights.

"I'll chase up there after that lot," said Wood. "You'd better get out and find a phone."

Bromley alighted, and the car shot away. The man on foot looked around for a telephone box, but did not see one. He crossed the road and turned left, thinking that he might sooner find a telephone in that direction.

He had walked two hundred yards when Austin 1800 YBC 8291 emerged from Brondesbury Road not twenty yards away from him. It went off toward Central London at a moderate speed. There was only one man in the car.

20

The Austin 1800 was not seen again that night. Chief Superintendent Coulson was disappointed, but not downhearted. The telephone message from Detective Constable Bromley was very helpful. Coulson looked at Kilburn on a big map of London and tried to remember the last time he had been in Brondesbury Road.

"I was around there not so long ago," said Sergeant Horne. "It's respectable, I suppose, but it looked a bit run down. Not the place where you would expect to find a big-time crook."

"That might be precisely why he has a house there," Coulson replied. "But as a matter of fact his choice might be a help to us."

Horne was doubtful. "There are a lot of houses on those little streets between Victoria Road and Brondesbury Road."

"And all more or less working class. How many do you suppose will have a telephone?"

Horne stared. "My word, that's an idea. Our boss smuggler is nearly sure to have a phone."

"Yes, and if there are half a dozen in that neighborhood I'll be surprised. We'll have a look round there in the morning and see how many there really are."

The *Dutch Girl's* return to her mooring was duly observed. The man who owned the rubber dinghy was followed to his home. The other two, identified as Quentin Mullen and Toffee Thompson, were allowed to drive away, but their car, a Morris Traveler, was seen again when it stopped for Thompson to alight near his flat in Bayswater. It was followed then, to a street in Hackney. Mullen entered a house there and left the Morris at the curb. It was subsequently found to be his own car.

At first daylight Coulson and Horne took a car and reconnoitered in the Brondesbury neighborhood. They noted eight houses with telephone wires and insulators. They also observed that the whole area, with its side streets between Victoria Road and Brondesbury Road, could be conveniently and unobtrusively picketed. They picked their spots and later set men to watch certain street corners. In this manner they ensured that no one could get in or out of the area without being seen.

Both of the Scotland Yard men had lost one night's sleep, and they expected to lose another. In the afternoon they were busy with the final arrangements for *Exercise Hoodwink*. Soon after the early nightfall of late October all their men were at their posts. Besides the exterior pickets around Brondesbury, every one of the small side streets was under observation, and special attention was given to houses with telephones. The homes of suspects in other parts of London were also under surveillance, with teams of men ready to resume the business of following them when they emerged.

In the darkness the shadowers were able to do their work without being noticed by the suspects. Toffee Thompson turned out for the evening and rode in a taxi to a small public house in Blandford Street. After an hour there he went to a nearby Angus Steak House, and after another hour he returned to the pub. He was not followed into either building because both were too small.

Lawrence Wilmot went to the Round Table bar in Charing Cross Road, and stayed only long enough to have one or two drinks. From the bar he went to the Palladium.

Quentin Mullen went to the White City greyhound track, and from there back to a small inn close to where he lived.

Jack Mayhew drove his Mini Cooper along the Fulham Road to Cranley Gardens. He waited outside a house there until a smart and handsome girl emerged and got into the car. The couple went to a restaurant in Frith Street, Soho, and apparently drank and dined there.

Whipper Slade went to an evening soccer match at Highbury. After the match he went to the Regent Palace Hotel and sat with a drink in the lounge for a while. Coming out of the hotel he met a young woman whom he seemed to know. After a brief talk he walked with the girl to a bus stop in Regent Street. They boarded a bus and rode to Notting Hill Gate. Alighting there, they walked to Westbourne Grove. The girl appeared to open the door of a house with a key, and Slade entered with her.

He left the house about half an hour after midnight, and walked the few hundred yards to his own lodgings. There, apparently, he went to bed. Learning of this, Coulson at the Yard was left with the unsatisfying thought that Slade was one *Hoodwink* suspect against whom there was no evidence.

Mullen left his local inn at closing time and went home. He stayed there, and probably went to bed at a normal time.

Thompson also left his Blandford Street pub at closing time. He hailed a taxi and rode to Kilburn Park, and alighted about a quarter of a mile from Brondesbury Road. He walked the rest of the way, and entered a house on one of the short streets which connected Brondesbury and Victoria Roads. It was one of the houses which had a telephone.

After the Palladium show, Wilmot had something to eat at a small, crowded supper bar in Old Compton Street. From there he walked to Piccadilly Circus and disappeared into the busiest underground station in London. His surveillance detail tried to keep him in sight, but whether by accident or by design he eluded them. However, a man answering his description was seen half an hour later entering the Brondesbury house.

About half past ten Mayhew and his girl friend left the restaurant in Frith Street. He took the girl back to Cranley Gardens and entered the house with her. But he stayed only a few minutes. Soon he was driving his nippy little car westward, and the police correctly presumed that his destination would be Hammersmith. He drove it into the yard of lockup garages there, and was in there for some time. The observers' guess was that he was filling up Jaguar XYL 4342 with petrol from cans. When he emerged from the yard at the wheel of the Jaguar he was not followed, on the assumption that he would now be so alert that it would be too dangerous. Anyway, the police had a very good idea where he was going.

It was midnight exactly when the Jaguar stopped outside the Brondesbury house. Immediately the man assumed to be Wilmot came out of the house, carrying what appeared to be two briefcases. He was followed by Thompson, also carrying something. They seemed to be engaged for a minute or two putting these things in the car, then Wilmot got in with the driver and Thompson returned to the house. The car went away. In Kilburn High Road it turned its back on London and sped northwestward.

Detective Sergeant Horne had been put in charge of the Brondesbury operation that night. After the Jaguar's departure the sergeant judged that it would be ten or fifteen minutes before Thompson left the house to make his way home: ten or fifteen minutes to make a phone call to Birmingham or Granchester or some other provincial city, to tell somebody that the diamond couriers were on their way. If he stayed longer it could be assumed that he had company, and that the house was not merely a meeting place and dispatch depot.

Actually Horne waited three quarters of an hour, then he telephoned Coulson.

"Should I go in, sir?" he asked. "I assume that our end of the job is finished except for the roundup."

"Well, you have your warrant," he was told. "Go in when you can. But you must be sure you can go in quickly. Don't give anybody enough time to make a phone call."

"I suppose I'd better wait until I can catch Thompson coming out. He won't be staying all night."

"Not unless he has a woman in there. Yes, I think you'd better wait."

So it happened that when the front door of the house was opened at ten minutes past two, Horne and a strong young C.I.D. man were on the steps, pressed against the wall on each side of the door. The hallway inside had a fairly bright light, and neither Thompson nor the man who opened the door for him could immediately see anything of the dark outdoors. Before they could, they were tackled by the two policemen, and other officers came running. The two were hustled back into the house, where there was a search of almost frantic haste upstairs and down to make sure that there was not another occupant who might be using a telephone.

There was no one else in the house, but obviously it was someone's home. A bachelor establishment, Horne guessed from the furnishings and atmosphere. He looked at Thompson's companion.

"Do you live here?" he asked.

The man was of medium height and build. He looked about fifty years old, with dark eyes and a very handsome head of white hair. In spite of the fact that he was wearing neither coat nor tie he looked distinguished. After a little thought he decided to answer Horne's question with a nod.

"What's your name?" the sergeant went on.

The man said his name was Peter Ventriss. Horne showed him a search warrant which had been issued after Coulson had made sure of the house. He relieved Ventriss of his keys and made sure that neither he nor Thompson was armed.

When he had done that he talked to Coulson on the telephone.

"All in order, sir," he reported. "I'm in the house and

I've got Thompson and a man who calls himself Ventriss."

"Very good. Send them here to me. You stay with a couple of men and see what you can find. If the phone rings, don't answer it."

Horne stayed, and searched. Among other things, he found some uncut crystals which he took to be diamonds. He thought they might be gemstones, but he did not know enough about such matters to be sure.

When Coulson heard of the find, he gave orders for a general roundup of all *Hoodwink* suspects. The London end of the operation was practically sewed up.

Jaguar XYL 4342 was too closely checked and timed for a switch of cars to have been possible. Because of this there were no bogus radio messages to make its driver turn from his chosen route. Again he avoided the motorway. He took the A6 and never left it. Men in concealment watched him go by, and it became evident that again his destination was Granchester.

21

It was a quiet night at the Tahiti Club in Granchester. Members and their friends had all departed before two o'clock. The entertainers had gone long before that. At two-fifteen the four-man orchestra packed up and left. The waiters and the hostesses went home also.

"All right, Sam," said André Vidor to the man who was assistant manager and bouncer. "You and Harry might as well go, and I'll lock up after you."

Sam departed with Harry the doorman. Vidor turned out the front lights and secured the front door. He returned to his office, where Donna Harlan and her half brother Roger were sitting. He looked at his watch. "Two and a half hours yet," he said.

"You go home if you like, Donna," Roger said. "I'll stay and keep André company."

"I'll stay," the girl said. "If I went home I wouldn't sleep."

"There she goes again, worrying," Vidor said. "There's nothing to go wrong. Here, have a drink."

As he poured drinks Roger said: "This consignment will stock me up for three months."

Vidor nodded. "That's right. We won't be having any more of these all-night sessions for a while. The next lot will go to Birmingham."

He got out playing cards, and the two men began to play tail rummy. When they had played a while Donna said: "Has Dixie Costello ever said anything about your getting a new car?"

"No," Vidor replied. "And if he did I'd tell him to mind his own business."

"He'll be wondering. About Rodge, too."

"Let him wonder. Rodge settled up with him long ago."

"And paid him good interest too," Roger said.

"You don't know Dixie," the girl persisted. "I'll tell you something. He has a line into the police station. He knows everything the bobbies know."

"And they know nothing, so all's well," Vidor retorted. "If they had any suspicions they'd be round here asking questions."

"They don't always work that way."

"I know *exactly* how coppers work. That's why they've never had me on their books."

"My God," the girl said, "how cocky can you get? I'm going home."

"Good" was Vidor's reply.

Donna alighted from a taxi at the end of the street where she lived with Vidor. She was walking the short distance to her door when a black Ford car stopped at the curb beside her. There were two men in the car, one of them in the back seat.

"Hello, Donna," the driver said through the open window. "Get in. I'll give you a lift."

"Thank you, Ned," she replied. "But I'm home."

"Not yet you aren't. Dixie wants to see you."

"What does he want?"

"Don't ask me. Happen he's lonely."

Costello's request was a command, and anyway the big man in the back of the car already had the door open. If she ran, he would catch her before she could get her key out of her purse.

"All right," she said, and got into the car.

At his flat in All Saints' Road, Costello was waiting. He had taken off his coat and tie and put on a white silk dressing gown, otherwise he was fully dressed.

"All right, Ned," he said, when his lieutenant Higgs ushered Donna into the living room. "You and the Dog wait outside in the car." And as Higgs turned to the door: "Sit down, Donna. What will you have to drink?"

She remained standing. "Where's your girl?" she demanded.

"She's gone home to mother."

"Gone for good?"

"I hope so."

"Well, *I'm* not going to stand in for her."

"Of course not. That's all in the past."

"What do you want, then?"

"Sit down. I want you to listen to a rather special tape I've had made. I think you'll be interested."

She sat. He brought her gin-and-water, knowing how she liked the mixture. Not until he sat down did she notice the tape recorder on a table beside his chair.

"Let's see," he said, bending over it. "I think you press this thing."

The spools began to turn smoothly, and Donna heard the beginning of a conversation. She listened in horror.

"You had us bugged!" she accused.

Costello stopped the tape. He was smiling. "Good, isn't it? I though you'd recognize the voices."

She was sick with dismay. "You had us bugged," she repeated dully.

"Only at the club," he said, in mock reproach. "I wouldn't eavesdrop on you at home."

"How *could* you do it?"

"I thought I'd better, when André seemed to be so well off all of a sudden. I've been in the club business a long time, you know. I know how to protect my own interests."

"Nobody has touched your interests. What we were talking about was none of your concern."

"I seem to remember you thought I'd be interested."

"I said you'd want to horn in."

"Very well. I'm horning in. It sounds like a good thing. Tell me about it."

"I can't. It'd ruin everything."

"*I'll* ruin everything if I'm not told."

"Dixie, please. Just leave it and talk to André about it."

"No. First of all I'm going to talk to you. You can tell me without André knowing. He need never know *who* told me."

"I—I can't tell you."

"Of course you can. I assure you, you *are* going to tell me. Be quite sure of that."

"André will kill me."

"André will be too busy with his own troubles. My partner. My pal. Using old Dixie for a front."

At four o'clock that morning there were more high-ranking officers in A Division Headquarters than there had been at that time since the Plumber case. The assistant chief constable and Chief Superintendent Clay were known still to be in the building. Superintendent of the Division Curtis was in the front office, and so was Chief Inspector Martineau and two or three inspectors. For the office staff there was no smoking and no light-hearted gossip. They were overawed.

Most of the senior officers were gathered in the open annex to the front office which was dignified by the title of Information Room. There were the switchboards and the radio installation, the maps, and the burglar-alarm board with the filed plans of vulnerable premises adjacent to it. It was nothing like the Information Room at Scotland Yard, but it was effective enough to serve the police of a city of a million people.

Among the front-office staff there were expressive glances and raised eyebrows when Curtis himself took over the main switchboard at half past four. But if anybody thought that Curtis would not be able to do the operator's work he was mistaken. During his long service Curtis had done every job there was in police work, and he had worked on the switchboard at a time when it was as likely to lay an egg as make a good connection and a clear message.

Curtis had no difficulty at all. When Jaguar XYL 4342 reached Granchester, it was checked through like clockwork, right to the Tahiti Club.

22

There were just four plainclothesmen watching the Tahiti Club; two at the front and two at the back. The observers at the back were watching from behind an upper window of a small dress factory, and they had a temporary telephone extension beside them on a cutter's table. They had a small but essential part to play in *Exercise Hoodwink*. Theirs would be the last message, reporting the Jaguar's arrival at the club.

The suspect car stopped beside the back door of the club at five minutes to five, and Detective Constable Kershaw at the dress factory reported the fact to Superintendent Curtis at A Division station. He added: "I can't see the number, but it's a dark-colored Jag all right. There are two fellows getting out."

Then Kershaw forgot that he was talking to a superintendent. He said: "Oy, what's up? There's another car, come the other way. It's stopped nose to nose with the Jag. *And* another car come to block the Jag in from behind. There's one, two, three, four, five men pounced on the Jag men, and they're belting hell out of 'em. They seem to be wearing stocking masks. Now one of 'em has grabbed a briefcase out of the Jag and he's run back to the first car with it. Another has gone with him. The other three have run to the second car. They're away. Both cars. One of the Jag men is sitting on his backside, holding his head. The other one has been laid out."

"The cars, man, the cars," Curtis rasped.

"Car number one with the briefcase is nearly white and looks like a Zephyr or a Zodiac. Car number two is another Ford. Cortina I think, dark colored. They went in different directions, number one toward Lacy Street."

Curtis left the line open while he spoke to the radio operator. Radio silence was now ended. He gave the description of the two cars, and said: "Give it to all cars. Get cracking. We want 'em at all costs."

On the telephone Kershaw was speaking again. "One of the Jag men is on his feet, and two fellows have come out of the Tahiti Club. The Jag man has gone to the car. He seems to be doing something to the back seat. Hello, he's got another briefcase. They must have given those bandits the dummy with the other one. Now they're helping the other Jag man to get up. They're all going into the club."

Curtis said, "Phew," and grinned with relief. He said to Martineau: "You got it? The hijackers have got away with a bag of sugar lumps." He turned to the radio operator again and issued an order to Detective Inspector Pearson, who since four-thirty had been waiting with a squad of men and two cars in a cul-de-sac off Bishopsgate. The operator repeated the order: "Surround and raid the Tahiti Club without delay. You should find at least four men and a bag of diamonds."

When that message had been given, Curtis sat back with a sigh, and brought out his pipe. "That's it," he told Martineau. "All we can do at present."

Martineau had been looking thoughtful. "I'm not so sure," he said. "How about giving those two Fords the no-approach treatment? You said: 'At any cost.' We don't want somebody to break his neck and ruin a good car for the sake of a bag of small coal."

"My word, you're right," said Curtis. He amended his message to motor patrols: "The Ford cars mentioned in previous message not to be intercepted. Report position and direction, and only follow if it can be done without being noticed." Then Curtis said to the switchboard man: "Get that through on the phones, too."

When that had been done the superintendent lit his pipe. When it was going to his satisfaction he said to Martineau: "I'd have thought you'd have been away to the Tahiti by now, to see what's doing."

The other man shook his head. "Pearson can handle that. I'm interested in those hijackers. It looks like typical Costello to me, and I don't get it. I had an idea he was up to the neck in the diamond job. But if he was, why the holdup? And how did he know?"

"The Harlan girl is one of his old popsies, isn't she? She could have been got at."

"Happen. But I can't see her doing the dirty on her own brother."

"Costello has ways of making people cough. He only needs a whiff and a whisper, and he can get the rest."

"Yes. Well, I'm staying here. There's just a chance we might get him."

"What with?" Curtis wanted to know. "A bag of nuts?"

Martineau did not reply.

The occupants of a police patrol car spotted the Cortina before the first radio message had been amended. Both cars went howling along Burleigh Street at high speed. Another patrol car appeared at a crossroads ahead, and was damaged trying to head off the fugitive car, which went through a shop window. Nobody was killed. Two policemen were injured, but the three occupants of the Cortina were injured more severely. Their names were Wolfe, Atkins, and Younger, and they were known to be members of the Costello mob. The Cortina was found to have been stolen from a private garage. The three prisoners were taken to hospital under guard.

The bigger Ford was allowed to go on its way without interference, and it was seen twice by police foot patrols who had been alerted through the winking-light telephone system. When the second of the two reports came through, Martineau said: "I think I know where that car is going, and I'm going too."

Dixie Costello answered the telephone at twenty-five minutes past five. "It's me, Ned," the caller said. "I'm where you said, and all's well."

"You got 'em?"

"Yes. In a locked briefcase. The old boy wants to be looking."

"Well, don't let him," Dixie said decisively. "*I'll* open that bag, and I'm on my way now."

Martineau had four of his own men standing by in the C.I.D.: Devery, Hearn, Cassidy, and Murray.

"Get the keys, Devery," he said. "We might have to go in somewhere."

All of them were tall, broad-shouldered men, as were most of Martineau's squad. They crammed themselves into a C.I.D. car, and Devery drove as directed toward Lea Park.

"We're going to call on a certain Aaron White," Martineau announced, but he told Devery to stop the car in a quiet street a good five hundred yards from Melbourne Villas where White lived.

"We'll walk from here," the chief inspector said. "Bring those keys."

Those were not the only instructions. Murray was told: "You've been to White's house. There's a back yard with a high gate, isn't there? You push on ahead, and scout around with great care, but don't be around there much more than a minute. I want you to find out whether or not there's a white Ford Zephyr hidden in the yard, that's all. Come away then, and you'll find the rest of us waiting at Lea Park School."

Murray loped silently away, a running shadow. The others walked to the school, which stood in its own playing fields in Melbourne Road, directly opposite to Melbourne Villas. The building was two stories high, and fairly modern. The four detectives climbed over the boundary wall of the playing fields, and walked in the shadow of the wall to approach the school from the rear. When they reached it Martineau said: "Find a door you can open, Sergeant. We're going to trespass but nobody will ever know."

Devery started work with the keys on the first door he found, and in five minutes he had it open.

"Good," said the D.C.I. And then rather anxiously: "Murray should be here by now. Go to the corner and look out for him, Hearn."

Hearn went away, and returned almost immediately with Murray.

"Well?" Martineau asked.

"There's a car in the yard, sir. A white one. It looks like a Zephyr."

"Anything else?"

"No, sir. I didn't linger."

"Anybody about?"

"I saw nobody."

"Fine. Now let's get inside. We shall have to grope about without lights."

On the other side of the door was a typical school corridor, with classrooms on both sides. The corridor was not too dark for a man to see his way, because it was glass-walled for the most part, and the classrooms themselves had big windows.

As Devery groped to find a bolt to fasten the door he had opened, Martineau instructed Cassidy and Murray. "Find the stairs and get up above here where you can overlook the playing fields. And no smoking. When you see anything worth mentioning let me know. You'll find me upstairs too, in the room most directly opposite to White's house. Is that door fast? Right. Devery and Hearn come with me."

The policemen went to their posts and waited, silent and still. Martineau and his companions had waited ten minutes when Murray appeared.

"A man on foot," he reported in a low voice. "He came along under the wall the way we did. He was heading directly here when he passed out of our sight."

"That'll be our sly fox, casing the school," the D.C.I. breathed in reply. "We should see him in a minute."

He looked out the window, straight across at White's house. It showed no lights. Looking along the side of the house, he could see the closed back gate, silhouetted against a street light nearby in the back street. If anyone opened that gate, or climbed over it, the movement could be seen from the school window.

"Here he is," Hearn whispered urgently, as he craned at another window. "Going down the wall side."

The others saw the dark figure, moving down toward Melbourne Road. Here at the front there was a stretch of lawn and flower beds, and ornamental railings facing the road. The figure went along the wall side and climbed out of the school grounds at the corner where wall and railings met.

"That's my boy," said Martineau happily. "That's Dixie all right. He'll be floating around for a minute or two yet. You go back, Murray. Get Cassidy and wait for us at the door."

The prediction was accurate. The dark figure moved cautiously, not hurrying at all. Dixie Costello always took as few chances as possible. He went right round Melbourne Villas, stopping frequently to peer into the shadows. Then he went halfway round again, and the watchers saw the shape of him as he climbed over the back gate of White's house and dropped into the yard.

"That's it," Martineau said urgently. "Let's move. No time to waste now."

Leaving the school, the five men went around the end of it, and climbed out of the grounds at the corner farthest away from White's house. From there, the end of Melbourne Villas, Martineau sent Cassidy and Murray creeping along the front, with orders to crouch below garden-wall level somewhere near White's front gate. With the other two, he went round the back. They climbed a wall where the leaves of a few shrubs over-hung it at the corner of the yard.

The yard itself was partly a small back garden. There was a wide asphalt drive and an open brick garage, but facing the back of the house there was a small lawn and a border of shrubs. There were three steps up to a little terrace and a French window facing the head of the steps.

The first light of dawn was showing above the roofs to the eastward, but there was no morning breeze. Everything was quite still.

Martineau looked, and saw a white car in the garage. Motioning for his companions to stay on the grass at the foot of the steps, he went carefully up to the French window. He peered down as he did so, seeking to avoid twigs and dead leaves. At the window he put his face close to the glass and looked down, and saw strips and spots of light at the foot of the dark, full-length curtains.

He listened, and heard voices. Then one voice said impatiently: "All right, Aaron. It might be a deal. Get the case open, Waddy."

There was silence, for perhaps half a minute. Then there was a shout, and Martineau knew the voice well.

"Pebbles! Bloody pebbles! I'll kill somebody for this!"

A French window was no deterrent to a man of Martineau's physique. When he heard those words, in that voice, he stepped back and then charged. His left shoulder struck where the two leaves of the window met, and a loud crack gave warning that the framework had splintered. He stepped back again and used the flat of his right foot to kick the window open, and a second later he had parted the curtains and stepped into the room beyond. Devery and Hearn followed him.

He found himself in a big living room. Besides a dining table and a sideboard, there were armchairs and a settee. On the polished top of the table was a brief-case. It lay flat and it was open, and brown pebbles were scattered over the table and on the floor.

There were four men near the table, and Martineau's

entry had been so quick and startling that none of them had moved from his place. The four were Dixie Costello, Ned Higgs, George Waddington alias Waddy, and Aaron White.

The expression on Costello's face had changed from anger to dismayed surprise, but this again changed to a convincing simulation of truculence when he saw Martineau.

"Hello," he said. "What the devil do *you* want?"

"You," said Martineau.

"This is a private house. You broke in. Aaron, ask to see the search warrant."

"I don't need a warrant."

"Have they changed the law, then?"

"No. It's as it always was. No warrant is necessary when there is danger to life. I heard a threat of murder."

Costello thought about that. "I ought to keep my big mouth shut," he said, and then added: "Well, you're here, but you've got nothing. Just a geological collection."

"What's there on the table will do for me."

"What? Pebbles?"

"The briefcase might be worth three or four pounds."

Costello was affronted. "You're going to arrest *me* over a lousy three pounds?"

"Three pounds or three thousand, it's the crime that counts. Highway robbery, with violence."

In the silence which followed that cold statement Aaron White had a chance to speak. "I have nothing whatever to do with any briefcase," he said. "I was asked to value some diamonds. I have seen no diamonds."

"You'd better come along all the same, Mr. White," the chief inspector replied. "We'll talk it over at Headquarters."

"This is the biggest mistake you ever made, Martineau," Costello declared. "I'll have the best lawyer in England."

"You can have any lawyer you like, after you've been charged and locked up. Sergeant, we'd better have the snaps on these three. Not Mr. White."

Costello's eyes glittered dangerously. "You're going to put the irons on *me?*"

"I'm going to do that personally. It's something which should have been done years ago. It you want to resist, that'll suit me fine."

"You're too old for the rough stuff," Costello scoffed.

"You're no chicken yourself. Now come on! Let's have you!"

23

Perhaps the most remarkable and gratifying result of the *Hoodwink* operation was the clearance of the Paddington murders. Coulson had no evidence against Whipper Slade, but when he learned that the body of yet another young woman had been found in a house in Westbourne Grove, he got in touch with Superintendent Ellaby.

Ellaby was still struggling with the murders, and getting nowhere. He at once called the men who had followed Slade the night before. They found that the house was the one which Slade had entered, and they identified the girl as the person who had entered with him.

Slade was found, and arrested. Ellaby sent the man's clothes to the laboratory. The material evidence he needed was on the underclothes: pubic hairs from the victim's body. He charged Slade with the murder, and then he began to collect his few witnesses in connection with the other murders, and he put his prisoner up for identification. He received enough corroboration of his suspicions to expect to be able to write off the other killings as the work of Slade.

"There you are, you see," he said to Coulson when he saw him. "You should have let me have a go at Slade."

"He'd have laughed at you," Coulson replied. "Now you've had him handed to you on a plate."

Coulson happily proceeded with his own investigation. Peter Ventriss refused to answer questions, but the detective surmised that he could get along without that kind of help. The diamonds found at the Brondesbury house proved to be gemstones, making it obvious that the smuggling operations had not been confined to industrial stones. Ventriss was identified as Pierre Vidor. At first little of interest was found among his papers, but in his ready reckoner there were two pages stuck together with a tiny spot of gum. On those two pages certain numbers were marked and underlined in a seemingly random way.

Coulson asked around: "Who understands codes?" It was not surprising in the Metropolitan Police that there was at least one man—ready for retirement now—who had worked on codes at the Admiralty during World War Two. This man, an inspector in the C.R.O., tackled the "code" and finally admitted that he could not break it. "But I know somebody who almost certainly can," he said. "And I think he'll be delighted to try."

So the puzzle was solved, and the code's meaning was found to apply to certain notes in Pierre Vidor's diary. Through them one Didier Vidor was investigated by police in Amsterdam, and found to have uncustomed gemstones in his possession.

Lieutenant Kropp and his colleagues were waiting

anxiously in South Africa, and Tiago Diaz was even
more anxious than they. Whatever happened, his position was dangerous. If the police were unsuccessful, his
accomplices would start seeking a traitor, because they
would almost certainly have been made aware of police
activity.

The information came. A person with the initials
"V.R." had communicated in code with Pierre Vidor
from various post offices in South Africa. It was possible
that "V.R." was a fourth Vidor brother. They closed in
on Raoul Vidor.

The Syndicate's agents had already spotted a "softy"
among the white overlookers in contact with Raoul
Vidor. They secretly grilled this man, and not being
policemen they were able to make promises as well as
threats. He collapsed and told everything. Eight white
overlookers on the Namil coast diamond field were systematically stealing diamonds during the sorting proc-
ess. The more difficult business of getting the loot out
of the diamond field had been solved quite simply: four
security guards had been corrupted. The investigators
settled the matter with equal simplicity. When they
were ready they arranged an unexpected double check
at the end of a work shift. They were able to carry this
through with so little disturbance that another double
check at the end of the next shift was equally unexpected.

Both operations were completely successful, and the
results delighted both police and Syndicate. Lieutenant
Kropp, now confident of promotion, had a feeling almost
of gratitude to Tiago Diaz. He gave him the warning
he had promised, and allowed him to sail quietly away
from Walvis Bay.

In London, Amsterdam, and Granchester the evidence against three more Vidor brothers was conclusive. Roger Harlan, Mayhew, and Wilmot were indicted along with André, Toffee Thompson went into the dock with Pierre.

Mullen and the Kew boat repairer were luckier. A Thames Police Court magistrate rejected the smuggling charges against them. He held that there was no proof that objects photographed on the *Dutch Girl* contained diamonds or that they had been taken from the *Ismail-baksh*. But the pictures proved that both men had used the boat, and they were charged with taking it from its mooring illegally. Coulson was not too resentful of their good fortune. He had got the men who mattered, and got them right.

In Granchester there was no evidence against Donna Harlan. She took over the job of managing the Tahiti Club, which now had a certain notoriety. The police noted that the club continued to do quite well.

The Costello mob was a shattered force. Six of them, including Costello, were remanded on a number of charges, of which the most serious was robbery with violence. Chief Superintendent Clay was of the opinion that some of the charges might have to be withdrawn, but nevertheless he was satisfied. There was enough evidence of enough offenses to make sure that the six men would be kept out of mischief for years. Costello had arranged for a high-priced defense, but it seemed impossible that he would escape conviction on the charge of receiving stolen property. And in view of the circumstances around that offense, it was likely that his punishment would be severe.

Surprisingly perhaps, Detective Chief Inspector Martineau had no comment to make about Costello's downfall. Except to his wife. At the fireside he told her that he had at last succeeded in catching a weasel asleep. At last Dixie Costello was in a place where he should have been a long time ago, and Harry Martineau could retire in contentment when he got his time in.